Love in the times of Online Dating

Love In The Times of Online Dating
Edited & Compiled by Priyanka Sahi
Print Edition

First Published in India in 2021
Inkfeathers Publishing
New Delhi 110095

ISBN 978-93-90882-11-3

www.inkfeathers.com

Love in the times of Online Dating

Edited & Compiled by

Priyanka Sahi

Inkfeathers Publishing

DISCLAIMER

The anthology "Love In The Times of Online Dating" is a collection of 21 stories by15 authors who belong to different parts of the globe.

The anthology editor and the publisher have ensured to make the content as reader-friendly and plagiarism-free as possible. Unless otherwise indicated, all the names, characters, objects, businesses, places, events, incidents- whether physical/non-physical, real/unreal, tangible/ intangible in whatsoever description used in this book are either the product of the author's imagination or used in a fictitious manner. Any resemblance to actual persons, objects, entities, living or dead, or actual events is purely coincidental.

The stories and poems published in this book are solely owned by their respective authors and are no way intended to hurt anyone's religious, political, spiritual, brand, personal or fanatic beliefs and/or faith, whatsoever.

In case, any sort of plagiarism is detected in the stories and/or poems within this anthology or in case of any complaints or grievances or objections, neither the anthology editor, nor the publisher are to be held responsible.

CO-AUTHORED BY

Deepanshu Joshi

Aastha Gupta

Priyanka Sahi

Ida Williams

Kristofer Bridges

Dayle Duncan

Khyati Bali

Lily Nielsen

Munmun Aidasani

Violet Evergarden

Amina Hazim

C.L. Williams

Ishika Jain

Nafisa Faruque

Ishika Jain

CONTENTS

Priyanka Sahi

Priyanka Sahi is a German Language Editor by profession and a writer by passion who loves to travel and explore new places in her free time. Being an avid reader she ventured into writing to explore her creative side, her journey started with writing blogs that eventually led her to writing stories. She already has one published story to her credit and 2 novels on Wattpad. She aspires to carve a niche for herself and gain her foothold in writing.

She can be reached @priyanka_writesandclicks on Instagram and priyankasahi@gmail.com.

EDITOR'S NOTE

Being a passionate reader I always dreamt of writing my own book one day. I ventured into writing when I was at a very low phase in my life, writing helped me in overcoming my emotional problems, it acted as a vent for me whereby I could tackle my emotions. This being my debut book will always be very special to me and I would like to thank Inkfeathers for making my dream come true.

I would also like to take this opportunity to thank my father Lt. Col. NS Sahi who left for his heavenly abode earlier this year but I'm sure he is watching over me from his new home. Dad I know that your guiding hand will forever be on my shoulder, you will always be the first man I ever loved and will forever hold a special place in my heart. Papa, you accepted me for who I was and loved me for the person I was striving to become, you always supported all my passions and I felt so protected in your presence, no one can take your place, you will forever be my daddy. I love you!

Coming to the Anthology- Love In The Times Of Online Dating gives you an insight into the modern dating scenario that is now prevalent in our society. I wanted to know what people feel about the modern era of dating and these stories do exactly that. I carefully handpicked each of these stories which depict modern love in their own special way.

This anthology got me in touch with a lot of talented young authors who are trying to gain their foothold in writing. While author hunting I not only got to interact with likeminded people but also made good friends on the way. The journey right from looking for co-authors to reading their stories and finally selecting the best ones has been truly an enriching experience for me. All the authors were very cooperative and they took all my suggestions very positively.

Lastly, I hope the readers will enjoy these beautiful stories as much as I enjoyed editing and compiling them.

1

Finding The Touch

by Deepanshu Joshi

It had been two hours since the alarm went off, but it doesn't feel like morning yet; lying, pondering, and staring at the ceiling fan - full of feelings and emotion, carried forward from last night. The circles under their eyes are as dark as the future of their relationship, yet there was still hope; for the world is not ending and certainly, there is a lot more to fight - love and cry over. The distance between them was nothing when compared to the space between them; they converse but don't talk, look at each other but don't actually see, they are together for a fair amount of time now, but are not actually there, with each other.

Once upon a time; relishing her Triple, Venti, Half Sweet, Non-Fat, Caramel Macchiato, scrolling through her mobile, Jiya was acting, as usual, to seem busy, to fish the world or maybe herself; reading the comments below her photo! Suddenly she saw a new name, appreciating her old beauty - a version of herself she no longer wished to relate to or think about; but certainly, that's not how things work! Curious as well as bored enough, Jiya felt this sudden urge to find out about this uninvited visitant in her life, and as she explored this guy's feed and in half-an-hour of sheer dedication and Macchiato fuelled earnest probing, Jiya knew

Anuv as clearly as couples know about each other after 6 months of relationship!

It was a bright sunny day, birds chirping - squirrels running - people laughing - life was happening at its same old fading pace. In the dimly lit room, on the 22nd Floor, sort of trapped in this concrete jungle; lying on his old mauve couch, he listened to his favorite indie-artist on-repeat. Anuv had lost his wife, Shweta, six months back in a severe bike accident; while returning back from their monthly fancy date; in a spree of whiskey-induced adrenalin, he lost balance of the vehicle on the damp road, hit the divider at 70km/h. He was holding on to the vehicle hence somehow didn't fall off it; his wife was only holding on to him, as alas! That had not been enough.

After spending the whole day outside, exhausting her social quota, Jiya felt as though lifeless, on her lilac couch, still wondering about Anuv? Jiya has not found any luck in the relationship department yet, hence any positive interaction with the opposite sex seems like a way in; a call-out to the 'damsel in distress' to finally come out of her cocoon and cherish the forbidden flavours of a realm totally alien to her. Jiya was not the most buoyant kind, rather she was a lot more fun to talk over text; once she was behind endless layers of filters and coats of nonchalant anxiety and periodic depression - modulating and adjusting, thinking and over thinking her silence, she is an epitome of sweetness.

Upon gathering enough courage to message him, Jiya finally sent a text, after typing and deleting, phrasing and re-phrasing the same line, not to look too upfront or fazed-out about it... "Hii" - she sent at 8:47 p.m. Then she got engaged in laundry & kitchen, getting low-key anxious about the reply; yearning not just for a reply but for so much more. Lost in his own horizon of lament and anguish, Anuv was still in denial of losing the love of his life. With each sunset, the memories of the accident haunted him to his very core, pushing him back inside his self-made cage of censoring, criticizing and inculpating his actions of that night and blaming it all on himself. Disrupting his routine, his phone beeped! As all his dear ones didn't bother him too much lately, he was annoyed and wondered who this could be, bugging him.

"Can't a man cry in peace" - he wailed as he unlocked his mobile.

To his surprise, this was Jiya's message. For a microsecond, Anuv felt alive; Jiya looked similar to his late wife! Getting a text from her and seeing that photo in the notification, worked like bliss in disguise for him; for a moment it was like Shweta was still there. Midway making two cups of tea, as he always did, for himself and Shweta, Anuv stopped and thought about all the logical scenarios he could, such as - who had texted him, and what was happening to him;

Jiya scrolled through his feed and dug into his pictures and memories, videos and reels; attaching herself to this new bond, living his moments through his photographs: low-key time travel. She finds herself drowning in a trance state, sitting too comfortably on her couch; relating so much with this girl on Anuv's feed. She sees this early 30's lady, distinguished features: beautiful smile, elegant eyes, roman-perfect nose, defined cheekbones, sharp jaw line and A-line symmetry of teeth. Shweta was literally Jiya incarnate; Jiya was shaking, it was as looking at herself and this freaked her out! Suddenly the lilac couch seemed a bit mauve to her. She saw all the posts of joy, happiness and of despair! She bit her nails a bit too deep that it hurt but couldn't stop herself while thinking of her action to contact Anuv. She felt a bit chilly on a warm summer evening, waiting for a reply.

Keeping aside the bizarre turn of events, Anuv replied:

"Hi, do I know you from somewhere".

Confused as he was, Anuv literally couldn't wait to take it slow and asked upfront! This was a bit over the top but it certainly matched the vibe of the moment.

Jiya got a bit offended but kept her hand on her pumping chest and took a deep breath. It was calm for a bit, Anuv could hear the wind blowing past his window as he eagerly waited for a reply. Jiya calmed her nerves, wrapped around her scarf around herself and switched off the main lights of the room & lit the fairy one. The dimly lit room complimented the start of this new bond. Anuv waited by the window, as if expecting for the winds to bring some message!

Taking a fair amount of time, Jiya replied to him. To their surprise, the conversation went as smoothly as if they had known each other. Both conversed till late night, as the fog cleared around them as well as in the air. Anuv who initially didn't realize the similarity in Shweta and Jiya, now could see that she not only looked like her late wife but she is a lot like her: her habits, her diction, instant replying to texts. He didn't feel like he was talking to some other person, for him, it was like - Shweta never left.

Anuv lived in Pune, while Jiya hailed from New Delhi. The distance as such was not the prior concern for them, but still was. They started talking on a daily basis and things paced as they do, and soon they entered the "AWW-Phase" of dating. No matter what stupid or big mistake one made, the other one only had one response to their actions! "AWWW"!

All this gave Anuv a false hope and he started believing that Shweta is back! Soon they moved to regular video calls; Jiya after analysing and talking with him for some days now liked the vibe and was taking it slow as she understood him. Anuv was not in a good place, due to the accident and whenever she talked with him over text or on video calls, she tried to be there for him, as a friend - comforting him, keeping him busy, away from the cage. Jiya saw this wonderful person - who had so much love to give, who wanted to laugh but just could not. She saw a person, who had lost the will to carry on. She saw in his broken smile; a wound so deep, which she could relate to on an emotional level. She could sense how hard it is for him to talk to some other girl, that too so soon. She could see in his eyes, longing for a hand to hold on to...

On the other hand, all Anuv could see was someone with whom he could share his pain, crack his lame jokes, be as awkward as he was! It didn't feel like he met someone new. It all felt so normal to him that while all the time that they talked; he thought he was talking to Shweta.

After a month of talking, getting fairly comfortable with each other, both of them decided to take this to the next step! They finally had their date on a video call; both of them got dressed and made the same dish, bought gin to celebrate the evening and sat at their favorite spots, while he sat on his mauve couch, Jiya rested on her lilac couch. She had dimmed the lights and lit enough candles to have a fair amount of brightness for the video call, while Anuv went for plain bright white tube light. Anuv wore a raven black shirt, while Jiya chose a Tuscan dress. The date went fine, and this paced up things, and they had more of these virtual dates.

For the first time, Jiya felt like she found what she was always looking for, and for Anuv it was like he found what he had lost. It was not like being on different pages, both of them were reading different books altogether. Yet, unaware of the doomed bond that was being made, both moved forward - clinging on to the momentary bliss that they felt. The very existence of the other, sort of completed them. It was as if they could finally breathe rest, sleep and live, the way they were supposed to.

Soon the Video calls became the new normal and they literally were in front of each other, all the time. For Jiya this was quite new but for Anuv it was something all over again. One day, while on another of their virtual dates! Anuv got a little over tipsy and got a bit more casual, not realizing Jiya was not much comfortable. As reasonable as she was, Jiya kept talking to him, understanding how difficult it was for Anuv, to move forward in life! She gathered enough courage and straightened up her spine, interrupted him, in-between one of his lame jokes!

"Anuv, I wanted to tell you something!" - she said, with a serious face.

Startled by this sudden awkward silence, Anuv got up and said "Yes, please do."

"I don't know how to put it, so I am gonna say it as it is" - she said looking down, adjusting the lock of her hair. Her heart pounded as what she was about to say was big and she knew it!

"What's the matter dear, it's me Anuv" - he said, in a little concerned tone.

"Anuv, I like this new phase that we are in, I love it actually" - she said, as her voice broke and her hands shook, not being able to look at him.

Anuv couldn't understand and there was a pause, he could hear the winds again...

When it was his turn to step up, he spoke what broke Jiya in unspeakable ways.

Anuv came a bit close to the camera and said: "Baba, what new phase are you talking about, it's what we have always had Shweta".

Jiya couldn't believe what she just heard! But realized what was going on! This feared the possibility of this happening, the initial days but forgot about it as things went pretty smooth. She disconnected the call and ran into her bathroom, feeling so stupid and vulnerable, and turned the hot shower on, and cried her heart out. Closing her eyes, she could see pictures from Anuv's feed of him and Shweta. She cried remembering how she imagined being with him, in those same places, enjoying those moments.

Under that hot shower, she felt his touch, a touch she could never feel, a touch her soul longed for, all this time, a touch she almost had but didn't. She turned the temperature warmer than usual, as tonight she needed it a lot more than usual..

2

Take Your Chance

by Aastha Gupta

PART I

I have been a Shah Rukh Khan fan all my life and that is probably why I could never imagine myself settling for an arranged marriage setup. I always believed in love and the idea of an arranged marriage irked me a lot. So when my mother brought a marriage proposal to me, I was disheartened and angry, both at the same time. Angry, because she knew I did not believe in the concept of an arranged marriage and disheartened, because I was single at that time and had no chance of falling in love anytime soon.

After much convincing from my mother and sister, I finally decided to give it a shot and started talking to an IT guy from Pune. Over the next few days, he told me everything about himself- his hobbies, his educational background and about the nature of his job. He was based out of Pune and was living with his friends and his parents were in Gwalior. He seemed to be a nice and genuine guy. While talking to him, I always had in the back of my mind that all the communication we are indulging in, shall determine whether we will get married or not. I kept thinking that marriage is the sole aim of this relationship and that freaked me out. My mother was also paranoid about it since the proposal came through my grandmother and she thought that she would be the one answerable to everyone in case things don't work out between us.

Everything was going fine until one day, I decide to give love a last chance.

PART II

Ishaan, a senior from school, replies to one of my stories on Instagram and we begin chatting.

***

Ishaan: "Looking hot in a saree". ;)

Me: "Haha. Thank you".

Ishaan: "Long time. How have you been"?

Me: "Yes, very long. Almost 9 years. But we never really spoke back in school. Did we"?

Ishaan: "Nah, not really. I remember you from school as the girl who had hot legs". ;)

Me: "Ahaaan. Trying to flirt"?

Ishaan: "You wish".

Me: "Hahahah. So how's life? I saw you were in Goa a few days back. How was your trip"?

Ishaan: "Oh, it was good. Goa is always good. What about you? What are you doing these days"?

Me: "I am a German language expert".

Ishaan: "Whoa. So are you into real-time translation"?

Me: "No, no. I work as an Editor with a publishing house. I have little to do with translation".

Ishaan: "Sounds interesting. I want to know more about it".

Me: "Only when we meet".

Ishaan: "Yeah sure. How about this Saturday"?

Me: "Umm. It's KKR's match this Saturday and I never miss their game. If you can look for a place that will air the match, I'm game".

Ishaan: "Oh, so I am talking to a girl who likes cricket".

Me: "Ya. So? Stop stereotyping".

Ishaan: "Hahaha. CHILL. Let me look for a suitable place then. Will ping you soon. Bye till then".

Me: "Bye".

PART III

Simultaneously, I was also talking to the arranged-marriage-guy due to family pressure. He was eager to meet me and was ready to fly from Pune to New Delhi as per my convenience. I, on the other hand, was quite skeptical about meeting him. I had my own reasons- What if our vibes don't match? What if he doesn't believe in love? What if he turns out to be a bore? What if he doesn't like to travel? All these questions started haunting me every day. Clearly, I wasn't ready for an arranged marriage.

Ishaan and I started talking over Instagram/Facebook at first. When we both got a little comfortable, we exchanged numbers and shifted to WhatsApp. With each passing day, we grew closer and WhatsApp chats turned into late-night phone calls. We both kept checking on each other from time to time. Our conversations were all heart-to-heart and not for once did I feel any disconnect with him. It was time for us to meet now. But before meeting him, I had to tell the truth to my mother.

"Mom, I'm talking to a guy called Ishaan these days. He is my senior from school and we have decided to meet tomorrow. Unfortunately, I will have to stop talking to the guy you introduced me to. He is a nice person but I'm unable to feel any connection with him. I feel I'm still not ready for marriage", I said. Without much drama, my Mom understood me and accepted my decision with an open heart. She asked me to be honest with the guy. And just like that, I texted him, "Hey, I'm still contemplating the idea of marriage and I think I won't be ready for it for at least, an year."

PART IV

"I will pick you up at 7", my phone beeped. I was ecstatic to meet him. Unfortunately, he got quite late due to the unforeseen traffic. Honestly, I was a little pissed. Hoping that the rest of the evening would be better than the start, I hopped into the car. We reached the place booked by him, it was a big bar in one of the malls of Noida. Since it was Friday night, the place was packed but we somehow managed to get a table on the terrace. Even though I am beer lover, I remember I had whisky that night, just to give him company. We ordered for 4 large pegs for starters. We both knew it was going to be a long evening.

We started talking about our respective school lives and why we never spoke back then. Of course we knew each other by names. We also spoke about travel. We both loved traveling and how! He told me about his aim of having 30 stamps on his passport before he turned 30. I was quite impressed, I have to admit. We spoke about cricket, movies, our favourite countries, my job, his business, our families, friends and what not. We gulped down more whiskey as we spoke and the evening finally came to an end. I was quite drunk by the time I reached back home. To my dismay, my mother was still awake. She immediately noticed that I was pretty much sloshed. That was the saddest and funniest day of my life. Funny, because I threw up in front of her and sad, because I got slapped by my mother at the age of 28. What a shame, I thought and passed out.

For our next meeting, I decided to invite him along with a bunch of friends. I remember we went to Nehru Place Social and there were around 15-16 of us (including friends and friends-of-friends). I introduced Ishaan to my friends and everyone hit it off with him instantly. He was the center of attraction that evening and everyone was curious to know the status of our relationship. Honestly, we had no clue ourselves. We just wanted to get drunk and know each other better. All good things come to an end like they say and so did that evening. While dropping me back home, he told me that he will be going to Mumbai for work the next day and then to South Africa, for a vacation with his family. I knew I would have to wait for 10-15 days to meet him again. But I needed that time to figure out what and how I felt for him. I guess we both did.

PART V

After a few months, we (Ishaan, my friend and I) decided to go for a small trip. It was like a weekend getaway to one of his favorite places- Marchula, a small town situated in Ramnagar, Uttarakhand. He loved fishing and this was his go-to-destination for Mahseer fishing. On our way there, Ishaan told me more about this unique hobby of his. I was quite fascinated to learn about it because I hadn't met an angler before. We picked up a few beers from a small shop on our way. All along, we kept switching between Coldplay and A.R. Rahman. Clearly, our music preference was quite dissimilar. Not only that, we had different tastes in food too. He could easily eat anything (or anyone!) under the sun and I loved my typical vegetarian food. I Loved to watch plays/theatres and he had never seen one. As they say, the best way to get to know someone is to travel with them. Around noon, we reached the resort. We had booked a small cottage for ourselves. We weren't quite tired since the journey was quite smooth. Hungry, we decided to order pakoras and coffee for a quick bite. We went for fishing the next day in the morning. Though I can't stand the smell of a fish but looking at the excitement on Ishaan's face, I decided to cheer him on throughout.

Movies, dinners, shopping, watching theater- that was pretty much what we did while we dated. We also visited Alibaug and Pushkar with our friends. We got to know each other better with each passing day when finally, he decided to tell his parents about our relationship. We went step-by-step since we never wanted to rush through anything so we decided to meet each other's parents separately before our families met. Hence it was a pretty smooth transition from the 'dating' to the 'to-be-married' phase.

We first met in May 2018 and by November 2019, we were married. What started off as a mere shot at love resulted into a lifelong companionship and commitment! These days he helps me in writing poetries while I help him plan his fishing trips. On some days, we listen to AR Rahman songs while having on-the-rocks whiskeys and on others; we swoon over Coldplay while sipping chilled beers. As someone rightly said, life is all about the moments we create and not about the milestones we achieve.

Ending the story on a very special poem that I wrote for him a few days back:

He is like an old Hindi film song-warm and cozy,
ready to embrace me forever.
New-age music can never replace his vibe,
For he is the only original tune left - his beats untouched.
Listening to him is like knocking on the doors of nostalgia,
reminiscing stories full of promises & regrets.
His soul is pure, his words melancholic
Standing by me always - in sickness, in health and in frolic!

3

Is This Love?

by Priyanka Sahi

The blaring sound of my alarm woke me from my slumber. Rubbing my eyes groggily I switched it off and rolled over to get 5 more minutes of sleep. This was my daily morning drill, quickly switch off the alarm and then sleep for 5 more minutes which eventually turns into an hour of extra sleep.

I finally got out of bed when I heard my mom yelling at the top of her voice asking me to come down for breakfast; I took a quick bath and made my way to the kitchen hall where my brother and father were already eating their breakfast. I greeted them 'good morning' and made my way to the end of the table. Taking a quick peep at my phone – I see 2 new messages from Stella

- "hey babe, meet me after the 1st class, have something important to discuss."

- "also, please do not forget to bring my top that you borrowed a month back, muah, see you"

The other message was from A., the message read –*"Hey beautiful, good morning! Call me when you see this, much love A."*

I should be excited seeing a message from my sweet boyfriend but I don't know why I have been getting mixed emotions lately. Andy and I have been dating since the last couple of months and apart from a few fights here and there we seem to be pretty good with each other, he's a good guy but I think we lack the chemistry. I have been contemplating whether we should just break up but it's so hard, I can't break his heart. "Earth to Tasha" my mom's voice broke my chain of thoughts, "eat your food sweetie, it's getting cold" before eating my breakfast I send my boyfriend a hurried text, "hey handsome, good morning to you too, I'll call you on my way to the university, got to go now, see you soon."

After breakfast I dropped my little brother to school and he annoyed me the whole way with his constant bickering. After dropping him I was once again lost in my thoughts, Andy and I have known each other since school but we started dating only a few months back, I like him a lot but I feel that the spark is missing, *"maybe I'm expecting too much out of this relationship"*, I tried convincing myself. I lost track of time with the nonstop introspection of my relationship and didn't realize when I had reached college, I was now parking my car in my usual spot when a guy stuck a small advertisement on my car's windshield. I got out and looked at the piece of paper, it was regarding a new book club, a quick glance and I shoved it inside my bag to read it later. I made my way inside; the corridors were buzzing with students, it was a usual morning scene where students were catching up with one another or hurriedly heading to their classes, I reach my class and get greeted by bright green eyes glaring at me, Stella gestured towards Andy who had been waiting for me.

Shit, I completely forgot I had to call him on my way here. Trying to make up for it I hastily kissed him and apologized, *"hey, I'm so sorry I forgot to call you, I was dropping my brother to school and he couldn't stop yakking, I just..."*, *"relax, it's ok babe, don't worry about it"*, he tried consoling me, here I was thinking he'd be mad at me but he's being all cute and leaving me bewildered.

After the first class I met Stella, both of us had this hour free so we headed to the cafeteria. *"So how are things between you and Andy?"* she asked out of the blue. I deadpanned, *"umm, umm"*; suddenly I was stuttering because I wasn't expecting to be thrown this question at me instantaneously, "th.. things are great, why you ask?" I mumbled and tried to act normal even though my heart was racing inside.

"Oh come on Tasha, I know when you're lying to me. You always seem so distracted around him, it's like you're being forced to be in this relationship, I don't know what's going on in that head of yours but be honest with him and let him know what you're feeling."

Stella is right I should not keep Andy in the dark, he should know about how I'm feeling. I gave myself a little pep talk and decided to talk to him after college today. The rest of the classes went by quickly, I was now in my History class which was the last lecture of the day and might I say a very boring lecture, I messaged Stella to wait for me outside the gate once classes were over, I needed a little thrust from the bestie to go ahead with the plan. After messaging her I placed my phone back inside the bag and my eyes fell on the crumpled advertisement, I thought rather than listening to this boring lecture why not utilize the time to read something I'm genuinely interested in. I placed the advertisement on my history book so my teacher doesn't sense that I'm whiling away time in her class.

The advertisement was about a book club that was being organized by this guy called Sam who happens to be a senior in the same college. We both knew each other but never really got the chance to interact. I was thrilled to read the details because I was an avid reader who loved books. Sam's number was mentioned at the end of the advertisement; I quickly yanked my phone out to store his number. "*Tasha*" I heard my name being called out by my teacher, *"could you please answer that?" "Shit shit, answer what? I've not even been listening to what she's been rambling about since the past one hour, what do I do now?"* I was just thinking about some clever excuses in my head when the bell went off. "*Saved by the bell*", that was close, I thought to myself. I let out the air I had been holding in and took a sigh of relief.

I was now driving back home and I recalled the conversation I had with Stella a while back outside the college. Stella is right I just need to be honest with him.

Back home I quickly made my way to my room; I tossed my bag on the sofa and literally threw myself on the bed. I was exhausted after an eventful day.

With my eyes closed I mentally planned my to do list, *message Sam- take details on the book club, call Andy-meet him and discuss things*, after a quick 10-minute nap I decided to first message Sam, he responded quickly and seemed like a great guy, he was very polite and patient with all my questions, we seemed to hit it off instantly. Getting rid of the thoughts about Sam I now focused on Andy. I messaged him asking to meet me at the central mall around 7 pm, he immediately replied with an ok.

Andy and I spent almost 2 hours at the coffee shop where I explained him everything that was going on in my head and requested him if we could take a break from our relationship just to see what we really want. He was upset at first and I could see him tearing up a bit but he controlled his emotions and told me he understands and respects my decision. I never thought Andy would be so mature and understanding, we agreed to continue being friends but I don't know if that would work out.

I messaged Stella that I took her advice and opened up to Andy and she replied, "*I'm proud of you babe, you did the right thing, I'll take more details tomorrow ;).*" Stella is more like a sister to me and I'm lucky to have a friend like her.

Once home I checked my phone and saw that Sam had added me to his book club on WhatsApp, I also had few personal messages from him, I quickly opened his messages without wasting any time

"So good to have you onboard, I will see you in college tomorrow"

"Also, just wanted to inform you that we have our first meeting this Friday after college, I'll share more details with you on this, goodnight 😊"

I don't know why reading his messages immediately brought a smile on my face. I mentally slapped myself for feeling this way; I reminded myself that I had just got out of a relationship and needed a break.

The next day in college was not very eventful, Andy and I met each other and since we had the same friend circle we had to act cordial. After the last class Stella and I decided to go to the nearby pizzeria with some of our friends, once we had placed our order my eyes fell on a familiar face, Sam was in the Pizzeria too with his friends, he noticed me staring at him and waved his hand at me lightly, I was so lost that Stella had to nudge me with her elbow to bring me out of my reverie. Sam approached our table in no time and greeted me and my friends, *"hey, Tasha, right? Nice to see you here"*, *"same here Sam, it's such a coincidence to bump into you like this"*, Sam and I were making small talk when our food arrived *"well let me not waste your time, please enjoy your meal, I'll see you at the book club this Friday."* Saying that he left to sit with his friends, I could notice Stella giving me a 'who the hell was that' look from the corner of the eye. Feeling embarrassed I muttered, "*I'll tell you later*" and looked away shyly; she didn't pester me but smirked with a glint in her eyes.

Once we were alone Stella kept on grilling me with questions about Sam. *"He's just a new friend, he has a book club and you know my love for books"* I tried explaining but she wasn't convinced. After dropping Stella to her house I reach back home and after changing into something more comfortable I lie down and check my phone, 2 messages from Andy, one from Stella and 1 message from Sam, I quickly opened the one that was from Sam. *"Hey, it was nice meeting you today, just to give you a little update, we were planning on discussing Pride and Prejudice hope you're ok with this book otherwise you can suggest something of your choice. Looking forward to seeing you at the book club – Regards, Sam"*

I waste no time and reply back saying it was a good book suggestion and I can't wait for Friday. I just realized that I had never been so eager to reply to any of Andy's messages while we were dating; Sam was giving me these quaint feelings that were so hard to explain.

The first book club meeting was highly successful; time flew by and in just over 2 months the club was thriving. Sam and I were messaging each other constantly, our WhatsApp conversations would last for hours into the night. We could talk about anything and everything, books being our favorite topic undoubtedly. Stella was sure I had fallen for Sam and I couldn't argue with her because of everything that I was feeling, the goose bumps which erupt as soon as I hear his voice, the feeling of euphoria when he's around, the erratic heartbeat, the eagerness to see him, I think I fell hard for Sam. Maybe this is what being in Love actually feels like. People spend their whole life looking for love but sometimes love follows you and comes in unexpected ways, all you need to do is keep your eyes open embrace it with open arms.

4

Until Then

by Ida Williams

She stared at the ceiling. It was always the worst at night. When the colors of the day had faded away and there was nothing left to do but try to sleep. Sleep. There was some twisted irony in that little word, an elusive state that seemed constantly just beyond reach. What of those spaces in the mind that are so well occupied in the daytime with work, people, talk and just about everything else that passes by? Now finally still and quiet, what comes? Not sleep, of course not. Perhaps that would be too predictable. Just a familiar feeling tugging away in the depths and the same bunch of thoughts flying around like demented pixies. No, naturally, not sleep.

She sighed and pulled the ear buds out. The music was not helping, too many repeats of sentimental tunes. She picked up her phone and swiped to turn off the song, squinting at the bright glare of the screen to see the time. It was really late. Turning over, she moved the pillows around, half the duvet falling off the bed in the process. There's always that thought that plumping up the pillows would somehow aid slumber. She lay back down, not bothering to pick the blanket up off the floor. The bed was ridiculously small even for a single.

The streetlamps were casting light through the blinds and a siren rang dimly in the city. Somehow the nights seemed longer recently than they had been before. Longer and restless. She kicked off the rest of the blanket. Was it worth lying there, or better to get up and do some work? There were still some final touches to put on the social media report for the morning. The morning. And the meeting was at ten. She squashed the pillow over her face. Oh for heaven's sake go to sleep!

In the darkness, the thoughts danced away again. A feeling that always sang the same tune. A lonely melody. It was an odd sort of loneliness, not one born out of a lack of family or friends or even isolation. It had no real cause to exist but there it was. That deep-rooted muffled ach. With a sudden force she sat up and threw her legs out of the bed and padded across the wooden boards. There was nothing else for it. It was time for tea.

***

He stared at the screen. The blank spreadsheets ran downwards, and the neon white light glinted on his glasses. The sound of the tapping keys echoed in the silent night air. One column filled. Tab down. Then another complete. Endless statistics, pie charts and engagement reports typed, and numbers entered. It had to be done, it was due in the morning. The phone vibrated in his pocket, reminding him of the time. An alarm set a few days before during the usual rush of healthy resolutions. He rubbed his eyes. It was late. Just a few more rows left. Thus, the alarm went unacted upon, as it always would do and as most of its predecessors had as well. Despite its majestic ringtone of upbeat bells, it had very little power. The keys tapped on. Such work was suited to the velvet depths of night. No people, no voices, no lights. No distractions.

A small gust of wind blew in through the open window dancing with the curtains, and a shaft of light fell briefly across the screen. He glanced around and moved up off the bed, setting the laptop down, and clambered over a pile of unpacked boxes to the window. Drawing the curtain aside, he peered down at the street below. The drug store light flicked red and the pizzeria blue, the little man in an endless state of tossing his pizza in the air. Up in the sky the culprit appeared again for a moment from behind a cloud. A slight piercing feeling edged its way round his subconscious and for a moment managed to flit in front of his eyes. He took a deep breath of the cool air and closed the curtain. The moon was bright that night.

***

She poured the hot water into her mug and spent a moment dunking the tea bag in and out of the liquid, watching it turn a pale yellow. Despite its benefits chamomile never looked very appealing. She turned off the kitchen lights and walked back into the bedroom, blowing cautiously onto her tea. Leaving the room dappled in the light coming in from the street, she walked slowly around. Perhaps some exercise would exhaust whatever lingering energy kept her awake. Silly really. She didn't feel energetic, just restless. Restless and thoughtful. Thoughts that were barely noticeable during the day seemed to thrive at night. The pacing continued round and round, as she took sips of the tea and felt the warm liquid rush down her throat. It had been a hard day at work and there was another one due in the morning. Stopping by the window she pulled aside the blind a few inches and gazed out. The moon was large and full.

***

He typed the last three numbers in and pressed save. After running an eye quickly down the page and seeing no glaring errors, he closed the laptop. Adjusting his posture, he stretched out his arms high above his head and rubbed the back of his neck. The sooner he unpacked and assembled the desk, the better late-night working would be. Picking up the computer he moved across the room and set it down on top of a pile of boxes next to the wall and plugged in the charging cable. Yawning, he looked around for the kitchen box. A hot drink would be nice. Stumbling around in the semi darkness, his big toe unfortunately soon made contact with a box. He muttered a few words under his breath and with a throbbing limb hobbled back to the safety of his bed. Leaning up against the side was the carry-on bag and inside a bottle of water. That would have to do. He sat down on the edge of the bed and rubbed his foot. It had been a long day. The flight that morning had been delayed and the couriers were late delivering the boxes. He opened the bottle and took a deep swig. A new city. A new job. Mineral water seemed an odd toast to make to a new beginning. A break in the cycle would be good. New faces. New challenges. New is often good. Rubbing his eyes, he drank some more. Those elusive but unapologetic thoughts wandered around once again and started drifting into his mind. Suddenly he felt alone, and the underlying sense of loneliness became more emboldened in the darkness. That would not magically change by moving. He drained the bottle and rather ambitiously picked up the wash bag off the nightstand but then instantly admitted defeat. It was too late, and he was too tired. Instead he just picked out his toothbrush. Taking out his phone, the light shining in front of him as he got up again. At least this time he could avoid injury.

***

Sitting back down on the bed, she drank the last of the tea and placed the cup down on the side table. She ran the brush through her hair several times, trying to get rid of the tangled feel and absentmindedly looked at the pattern of moonlight falling in from behind the slatted blind onto the floor. She had a dress just like this in the cupboard with crisscrossing lines and blocks. Her phone vibrated and a notification popped up on the dashboard. One of her friends working late, half smiling she wondered how many of them were awake there in the city at that hour. Her smile faded as she read the text.

Jake says you left coffee this morning. What's the matter? Didn't you like him? He's a nice guy.

She sighed and used her forefinger to tap the icons on the screen.

I know but he's not right for me.

No more stupid set ups. Sure, he was nice. Good looking, friendly and they had even liked some of the same shows. She laid her phone aside, her shoulders drooping over. There was nothing in him that made her feel excited or happy or anything really. Nothing that made her heart beat any faster. And frankly all he wanted was a girlfriend. Anyone to talk with. Anyone to be with. It didn't have to be her, any nice girl would do. Just someone to share some time with. Perhaps that was enough for him. She shivered and felt very much alone. There was so much more she wanted. Exactly what, was hard to put into a few words; a strong friendship, a passionate lover, a supportive partner. Someone who would make her feel special, make her feel very loved and someone who would become an essential part of her life. Someone to be with for a lifetime. She moved more onto the bed, feeling the springs bounce gently as she crawled towards the pillow end. Was anyone going to want that as well? The darkness swirled around her. Sometimes it seemed as if she was the only one.

***

He sat down on the side of the bed and ran his hand several times through his hair. The toothpaste he had picked up at the airport was really strong, even after gargling he could taste it. The phone screen lit up as a pile of unread messages wanted to make their presence known. Scrolling down he looked through the list of alerts, 20% off sale emails and movie recommendations, pausing his finger only to read one from a friend.

Just seen a cool profile on the forum. She looks great for you:) Get chatting!

Underneath the text was a link. Frowning he quickly thumbed a reply.

No thanks!

Hitting send he leaned back, flopping onto the mattress. He'd been there before. It wasn't worth it. Forums. Chatting. Swiping left or right. Searching, normally desperately, for someone. Anyone. He had tried that. It had often felt so empty. The more he had tried the worse it had become. Too many disappointments and people wanting nothing more than a fun time. So many things judged on appearance. Some people liked it, but he was so weary of it all. It was done. Over. The constant grinding check for messages and matches. Perhaps in the end love didn't happen on command. It came when the time was right. Not until then. He rolled over and grasped one of the pillows to his chest. Still he wanted someone. A woman he could have the best of times with, someone who thought he was cool… someone to love. Night-time surrounded him and the loneliness swept around unabashed. No amount of decisions could ever fully drive that away. It was easily beaten in the daytime when people and work took over. When there were bright colours and plenty to occupy the mind but there, in the dark, it danced away in earnest. He hugged the pillow tighter and closed his eyes.

***

She leant over the side of the bed, picked up the duvet and pulled it up to her waist, grabbing one of the pillows with her free hand. Somewhere along the way she had to keep believing that there was a man waiting out there for her. The world was large. Statistically there had to be someone. Was he near or far? The feeling of unhappiness wouldn't budge, and she tightly crushed the pillow in her arms. Perhaps if she focused hard enough, she could send some vibes away to where they were needed. She almost laughed at herself, sounding tired and ridiculous. Nevertheless she did it anyway. It was all she could do.

***

After a while his grip on the pillow lessened and he turned over. He needed to be in good shape for the morning. First day on the new job. A new office to go to. New co-workers to meet. Making a good first impression was always important. Yawning he drifted off. The right woman would come around one day. Someone supportive, loving and who would want to spend the rest of her life with him. And until then...?

***

She closed her eyes. The alarm would go off in a few hours and the meeting was at ten. The report had to be presented and the new team member was coming aboard. That was good, they had too much work already. A new hand would help a lot, they would handle all the statistics and engagement analysis. No, it was a "him". She vaguely remembered someone saying it was a "him". Settling deep into her pillows, sleep was coming at last. One day there would be a man who felt the same way. The man just for her. And until then...?

***

That bit of faith would have to do.

5

Luv N Pain

by Kristofer Bridges

Warning - This story contains explicit content, acts of violence, use of drugs, alcohol and aggression.

The story is in the form of a Novella that is divided into 3 Acts.

Act I

Let me introduce you to a man named Mac Bell.

Mac is 28 years old and well, Mac is whom one would describe as the Big and Tall type of guy. An African American standing a whopping 6 feet and 4 inches, weighing in at almost 300lbs! I mean the guy's built like a line-backer. Mac was your average high school Jock, he played a lot of sports and was very good at them. But all that came to an end when he broke his ankle in 3 places. An injury like that would be enough to end even the greatest athlete's sports career. After graduating high school, Mac got a job at his future father in-laws cleaning business; Dust Busters, where Mac has been working ever since.

This story ironically starts on a Friday late in the afternoon. The day was going normal as usual; Mac is at work listening to his favorite playlist as he finishes up vacuuming the inside of the library.

"Alright, and done!" He says as he takes an ear bud out of his ear and turns the vacuum off. "Now, the only thing left to do is to collect the trash from each room" he says when his phone suddenly goes off... it's a text from the boss.

Text: hey Mac, you've already reached your 40 hrs for the week. Go ahead and clock out and take the rest of the night off, Christian will pick up where you left off.

Cool Mac responds back. Wasting no time he then calls Karren, his wife of 5 years. But the call goes to voicemail

Before, I continue with this story, let me tell you about Karren.

Karren Bell is also an African American, standing tall at 5'6." She's built in the right places and is a very pretty girl and she knows it. The two were high school sweethearts and got married a few years after graduation, immediately after turning 21.

Now back to the story.

"Damn it" he says to himself as he hangs up the phone. "I hope she still isn't mad at me, he says to himself as he heads to the bathroom to wash up."

You see, Mac and Karren got into an argument the previous night. The argument was over money and ended with Mac sleeping on the couch.

"I'm going to just send a text" he says. As he lifts his phone up and begins to text Karren.

After leaving a message Mac gets into his car and leaves. As Mac gets on to the highway he grabs the rest of the blunt he rolled and lights it.

"I just hope she's not too mad at me" he says to himself as he exhales the smoke and speeds down the highway doing 70.

"I know I messed up ok. I can own up to that, yes I blew the money to help Maria out. But that was it. It's not my fault that I'm attracted to her as well" he continues talking to himself... the exit approaching in half a mile. "I just can't help but wonder if she might be cheating on me again" he says. "She's acting very much the same, I forgave her the first time but if she is doing it again, then I don't think that I will be able to forgive her this time around. And I pray it's not with that same nigga Chris because if it is" he says as he firmly grips the steering wheel. "I'm going to jail for murder, in the first degree."

A few years ago Mac had caught Karren talking to another man on Facebook! This incident took place only four years after their wedding! Now before you get the wrong idea let me paint a picture for you, it was 2008 and Times were tough with the rescission sweeping the nation as well as the swine flu pandemic going. Gas was steady on the rise, the economy was down, and many people were getting laid off. The money began slowing up and the bills began piling up for Mac and Karren and this caused a strain on the two's relationship. One day while Karren was in the shower Mac decided to go through her phone. So he opens up Karen's Dm on Facebook and sees that this guy Chris was going to send Karren $1200 if she would be his adult entertainment for the weekend at his beach house. After reading that Mac does what any man would do.... he snapped and started punching holes in the wall. When Karren got out of the shower to see what the hell was going on, she was shocked to see the door wide open with holes in the living-room walls, her phone on the floor with the message open and Mac was nowhere to be seen. The two were separated for 4 months after this incident.

"Shit I left her ass before", he says as he inhales the last of his blunt. He holds it for a brief moment before exhaling. "And I'd do it again" he continues on rolling the window down tossing the roach. A few minutes passed and Mac gets off the exit ramp and comes to a stop at the red light. He then sits back and just stares at the gas station in front of him.

He sighs. "I know I shouldn't be doing this" he says as he turns his steering wheel left to get into the turning lane. "But I'm a grown ass man" he says as he looks both ways before driving across both streets to get to the gas station.

The Gas station is only 5 miles up the street from Mac's residence. He puts the car in park and checks the time, its 8:45pm.

"I'm just going to park right here" he says as he pulls up and parks right out front. "Now let's see what the hell I'm going to be drinking on tonight", he says. He gets out of the car and hits the alarm. Mac enters the gas station and heads straight to where the coolers are. He stops and stares at the selection. "Hmmm I think I might just get these," he says as he grabs two 16oz Naddy Daddy cans. He then looks over at 42oz Naddy Daddy. "Fuck it, I'm gonna get this too." He says as he grabs the 42oz can. I'm going to be sleeping on the couch anyways. He says as he shuts the door and makes his way to the register.

"Sup bro" Mac says to the cashier.

"Hey Mac" the young cashier says back "what's been going on with ya" he says to him as he rings him up. "It's gonna be 4.58$"

"Mark isn't coming in today" Mac says as he opens his wallet and grabs his red bank card and swipes. Ding.. Mac goes to put in his pin.

"No" the cashier says. "He called out earlier he said his stomach hurts and he had diarrhoea".

"Really" Mac says as he snatches his card out of the machine. "I hope he don't have that Swine flu shit".

"Me too. But that's why I picked up this job, to help my family out during these tough times."

"I respect that" Mac says to him as he gives him a knuckle bump. "Yea do all you can because this recession is real and it is tough, but we will get through it." "I had seen something on the news about a $250 stimulus check being sent out at the beginning of next week though"

"Yea, I had heard the same, but my mom won't qualify for it though. From what she was telling me, the $250 stimulus will only go to people on Social Security, Supplemental Security Income, veterans, and railroad retirees."

"Damn that sucks. That's the government for you giving money to the wrong people."

"Aint that the truth, and during a recession at that."

"Now you're getting it. But At least your mother will receive that tax cut for her taxes."

"Yea, I had forgotten about that."

"Ya, see kid doomsday is coming and when the world turns into World War Z then I'm just gonna be glad I own a gun" Mac says as he grabs the bag.

"Are you a doomsday prepper?"

"No but I am a God-fearing man who believes in the end of days."

"Amen to that."

"Stay up lil bro", he says to him, "oh, and tell him I stopped by" he says to him as he exits the store.

He jumps in the car and takes a deep breath and holds for a brief second blowing it out completely. "I'm going to try again" he says as he reaches into his pocket and pulls out his galaxy and calls his wife. Again no answer, finally he shoots her a text.

Text: Hey babe! Want something to eat?? Your dad gave me off and I'm out.

He then sits back, turns the radio on and opens the first Natty Daddy and begins to drink it waiting on her reply. The time is 8:57pm.

After finishing the Natty Daddy still no reply. So he pulls off and heads to the crib, his house being only 10 minutes away.

As he pulls up to his house, he notices a 2008 Maserati Gran Turismo sitting in front of his house.

"Whose car is this parked out in front of my house", he says to himself. It's probably the neighbours from across the street. I'm done telling them to stop doing that shit, he continues on. As he gets closer to the house, that's when he notices it.

"What in the world!" he says as he pulls up to his house, flicking his high beams on to get a better look at the car. "No Way!" He says out of pure excitement "that's a fucking Maserati!" wasting no time he pulls into the driveway. He parks the car and jumps out. I'm gonna definitely take a few pics. Ha I'm gonna even put them on Facebook, people are gonna think it's mine. Mac takes about 10 pics before he heads in.

As he goes to unlock the front door, he sticks his key in the lock and finds that it's unlocked. As he enters the home he smells dinner cooked and loud music coming from the bedroom.

Karren! I'm home! "he yells as he shuts the door."

"Karren I'm home" he yells again as he locks the door." "That shit smells good" he yells as he puts his bag down. Suddenly he notices a pair of shoes by the couch. He then goes over to the kitchen only to see the food has already been eaten and there are 2 plates in the sink. "OH HELL NO!" he says. Wasting no time he heads back over to his bag. He unzips it and pulls out a revolver "Karen" he screams out with the gun in his hand as he heads into the bedroom. He opens the cracked bedroom door.

"Karren!" he yells. As he enters he looks around and to his surprise there's no one! The bedroom is clean with the bed neatly done. Karren then steps out of the master bathroom,

"Yes?" Karren says nonchalantly .... "You're home early, and why do you have a gun in your hand she yells, what's your problem?"

"Woman I know there's another man in this house" he says glaring at her.

6

Luv N Pain

by Kristofer Bridges

Act II

What are you talking about"

"KARREN THERE ARE SHOES IN THE LIVING ROOM WHERE I SLEPT LAST NIGHT. HE THEN COCKS HIS GUN AND THOSE AIN'T MY DAMN SHOES!!"

"Calm down, she says, I bought those shoes from a person I met on Offer Up. I know that you have wanted a new pair of shoes since long and look at how childish you're acting" she says staring at him.... "I bet you were smoking and drinking again WERNT YOU?!.... And don't lie" she asks him as she folds her arms.

Mac takes a minute to think as he looks around. He then drops his head. "Yea" he said. "I guess I jumped the gun a bit."

"A Bit" she says.

"Yea but it was only because you weren't answering my calls or texts!"

"Yea coz I was in the shower" she says as she puts her hand on his cheek. "You always act like this." They then stare at each other.

Mac takes her hand and holds it "look let's not do this. I'm just gonna apologize."

"No don't". Karren says as she cuts him off. As she yanks her hands from his grip and stands up. "It's my fault, like I said before I was jealous and envy got the better of me." She tells him as she turns around.

"Let's just drop it" he says as he stands up and grabs her by her hand turning her to face him.

Mac then bends down to kiss Karen.

"Another reason is because I saw that Maserati sitting in front of the house. I'm sitting here thinking that you done got with a celeb or something" he says in a chuckle.

"A CELEB!" She says and they both laugh.

"Come let me show you" he says. And they both head towards the front door. They get to the living room and Mac decides to turn around and cut the music off.

"One sec. Let me turn this radio off" he says. "Wait, no Mac wait, wait!" Karren screams.

And there he sees it; a naked man with his face covered running from the closet to the open window.

"You lying bitch" he screams as he pulls the gun and fires 1 shot missing his target by a hair. The man jumps out the window and heads towards the Maserati.

Mac runs after him "I'm gonna kill that fucka" he yells. But before he can exit the bedroom Karren stands there blocking him from leaving.

"Move Karren", Mac screams as stands there.

"No. I don't want anything bad to happen."

"Bitch I said move", he says as he bulldozes Karren.

Mac reaches the front door and sees the Maserati, Mac begins to fire again! Bang bang bang bang.. hitting the Maserati multiple times. He then runs out on his lawn and continues shooting firing only a few shots before the car is out of range.

Damn it he yells as he jumps up and down before storming into the house and slamming the front door.

Mac goes straight to the refrigerator and grabs his 42oz Natty Daddy and goes and sits on the couch and turns the TV on and takes a sip.

Karren is standing in the kitchen.

"Mac" she cries out, but no response. "Mac", she calls out even louder this time but all he does is sip his Natty Daddy and turns the TV up.

Karren walks into the living-room and stands in front of the TV. "Mac!! I know you heard me calling you."

"Move Karren", Mac says very calmly sipping his drink. I'm not gonna ask you again.

Karren then walks over and sits on the couch next to Mac staring at him.

"Mac" she says.

"Save it Karren" Mac says interrupting her. "I don't want to say anything until the police get here.

"So what are you saying? You don't want to talk to me."

"What is there to talk about Karren. Oh wait I know let's talk about who the fuck that was jumping out of my window naked!!?" He says as he puts his gun on the arm of the couch and lights a black and mild.

"I know it looks bad but just hear me out."

"What is there to hear out!? I fucking seen someone running out of my closet, and I know I don't keep naked men in there."

Suddenly a knock is heard.

knock knock knock. Police

Mac then gets up and opens the door. "Good evening officers." He says as he greets the two.

Yes we got a call of gunshots being fired from this address.

"Yea its true" Mac says. "It was me. My wife was having an affair and I tried to kill the person. I can show you the gun and paperwork for it."

"Yes I would like that." The officer says.

"May we come in?" the other asks.

"Sure" Mac says and lets the policemen in. He shut and locks the door behind him.

The police glances around, "nice place you got here."

"Thanks", Mac says.

The officers then look at Karren. She's on the couch in the fetal position crying with a black blanket covering her.

"So you must be his spouse", Karren looks down.

Mac then interrupts them. "And this is the gun I used," he says as he goes for the gun.

"Sir!" The officer says sternly. "Could you not go for the gun? Me and officer Davis can handle this part" officer Briggs tells Mac.

Mac smiles, "sorry about that."

Officer pulls out some latex gloves. "No biggy", he says as he walks over and picks up Mac's gun.

"I believe I fired something like 5 shots," Mac tells them.

"I understand", the policeman say. He then looms at the man, well then would you like to press charges on your wife or get a divorce.

Karren then looks at Mac.

"Nooo, Mac honey, don't. I love you."

"Love me. Karren don't play dumb! This isn't the first time you've done something like this. I told you before, if you were to ever slip up and do something like this then it's over between us."

"Mac"! She cries out. I'm sorry. I truly am. She says as she sobs. Please don't leave me. I.... I... I need help. Please Mac", she begs out as she sniffs. "Please."

Mac looks at her. He then turns and looks at the officer. "If I do, I'll call you guys", he tells officer Briggs and then shuts the door and locks it.

Karren sits there just staring at Mac.

"You won't even look at me," Karren says.

"That's because I can't", Mac says continuing to stare at the TV. "This isn't the first time you've done something like this. And what made it even worse was", he turns to look at her "That even after you were caught, you still lied about it..... I just can't believe you...I don't want to be with you under the same roof."

"Don't say that she screams out in an emotional state. Look I know I messed up. But you must believe me when I tell you I love you."

"Believe? How? When every time I turn around I catch you doing some hoe shit!"

"Because I'm pregnant!"

Mac pauses. "Now... now is the time you choose to tell me this." He yells as he stands up and punches a hole in the wall. "How do I even know it's mine?"

"Because..... You're the only person I have unprotected sex with." She then pauses.

Mac turns around and takes a deep breath. "Who was it?" He asks.

I can't tell you."

"Karren! You are MY WIFE! And if you want to make this work then you gotta tell me the truth. Because I swear to God! If it was that nigga Chris from last time then I'm sorry but his ass is grass. Now tell me because I'm not going to ask again."

"Ok" she says wiping the tears from her face, but you must promise me that you won't do anything crazy."

Mac pauses. "Ok I promise, now tell me."

"Ok." It was Mark from the gas station." She almost whispers and looks down.

"Seriously!!!!!! COME ON KARREN", he yells as he punches the wall making another hole there..... "Why him.... I was just in there."

Look I gotta wake up early. Can we finish this later." She says as she walks over and kisses him on the cheek. She then turns around before shutting the door. "Would you like to come to bed with me"?

"No not tonight." Mac says. "Just give me some time for myself."

"Alright", she says as she shuts the door.

Mac then picks up the phone and calls his father-in-law.

"Dad", he says. "I'm gonna need tomorrow off."

"Sure, is there something wrong"?

"Yea.... I caught Karren cheating on me."

"What.... That damn girl. I'm gonna call and talk to her tomorrow. You go ahead and take the day off."

"Cool, and thanks dad."

"You're welcome."

He then gets on Facebook and begins to make different posts.

The next morning Karren wakes up for work and gets on Facebook and begins to scroll down her timeline and read some of Mac's posts. She comes out and sees Mac in the same position.

"You ok"? She asks him, but gets no response. "Have you been up all night"?

"Yea I couldn't sleep."

"Look I know I messed up, but I don't want to lose you. You're special to me." She says to him as she kisses him on the forehead. "Got to go now, but we're gonna finish this later today when I get home." Love you, she says as she shuts the door.

Mac checks the time. Its 6:30am. He rolls his last blunt and smokes before falling asleep.

When he wakes up its 10:30am, he texts his childhood friend Tony to come by as he wants to buy a gram and he needs to tell him something. He then texts his OG the same message.

"I might as well go and get some brew", he says as he stands up. "I still can't believe this shit", he says as he walks out the house to get in the car. "I better go to another place to get this because if I go to the gas station and he's there then I'm gonna kill him", Mac says as he backs out of his driveway. As Mac passes the gas station he simply ignores it.

Mac goes to another store to get his beer. While coming back Mac stops at the light right in front of the gas station. He looks over at the gas station and clutches the steering wheel, I got half the mind to shoot up his car, and he gets a text from Tony. "Pulling up." Mac texts back down the street. The light turns green and he peels off.

As he gets back house, Tony is pulling up behind him, he blows the horn.

"What up nigga", Tony yells from out the window

Mac throws up the deuce. They get out and dap each other up.

"Man I gotta tell you some shit", Mac says as he walks over to unlock the door.

"What's up"? Tony asks as he steps inside and closes and locks the door. I saw that crazy shit you were posting on Facebook.

Mac sits on the sofa and grabs a can of beer and pops the top. "I caught Karren cheating on me last night bro."

7

Luv N Pain

by Kristofer Bridges

Act III

Mac passes Tony the 20 dollar bill.

What! Tony says stunted in disbelief reaching into his pocket. No way. He says as he pulls a gram size bag of weed out of his pocket and hands it to Mac.

"Yea bro", he says as he takes the gram from Tony. Mac then takes a cigar from out of the bag and begins to bust it open to gut it.

"Pass me a beer and the other cigar bro. I want to hear this shit."

Mac passes Tony the cigar and beer.

Toni cracks the can open and takes a gulp... "ahh ok", he says as he sits back and begins to split his cigar. "Ok, go ahead," he says to Mac.

By this time Mac has already rolled his blunt and is just about to light it. Mac hits it and begins to tell the story. About half way through Mac gets a knock at his door.

Knock knock knock. "Yo Mac it's me lil bro." A voice cries out from behind the front door.

"Shit you called OG"? Tony says as he gets up and opens the door.... "What's Popping OG", he says as he extends his right hand and greets OG.

"Sup Tony", he says as he daps him up and walks in. Tony shuts and locks the door behind him. "Sup Mac", he says as he walks over to him.

"Sup OG", Mac says as he stands up and daps him up and passes him the blunt.

"Shit bro you know me," he says as he inhales and holds it for a brief second. "Just been staying out of the way, but what's up bro, everything good?" He asks as he takes another hit.

"No bro." Mac says as Tony passes him the second blunt. Mac takes a hit.... "I caught Karren cheating on me last night." He says as he blows the smoke out.

"Damn bro", OG says as he passes the blunt to Tony.

"That's what I had said OG", Tony says as he hits the blunt. He just told me a few minutes before you walked in.

"Damn", OG says again as he grabs a beer. "And you said this happened last night?" He asks as he opens the beer and begins to drink.

"Yea", Mac says blowing the smoke out. "The nigga was hiding in the closet OG, he came out when he saw us leave. So as I'm turning around to go back, that's when I saw him....and I shot at him."

"My Man"! Tony says with a smile. Did you hit him"?

"No I missed both shots", Mac says as he hits the blunt again.

"Too bad, did you see who it was"? OG asks

"Hell no OG, the nigga was wearing a facemask, shades and a hat. The only thing I know is that he was a nigga"!

"Wow. In your own crib fam", Tony says passing the blunt.

"Exactly, and you want to know the kicker?" Mac says as he chugs the rest of his beer and opens another.... "The bitch said she's pregnant! Congrats to me", he yells spastically, as he begins to chug the beer.

"Damn bro", Tony says as he puts his head down, "that's tough bro."

"Yea, is the kid even yours little bro"? OG asks.

"She claims it is OG, but after this... it's got me thinking if she's lying because this isn't the first time I've caught her sneaking around, it's just thc first time I seen another person. A few years back I'd seen a dude named Chris trying to pay her for sex."

"What"! OG says.

"Yea I remember you telling me about that", Tony says.

But after talking to Karren she told me who it was.

"Who"? Tony asks.

"My man Mark from the gas station"!

"Time out, you mean that one nigga you introduced me to a few weeks ago who was trying to buy some weed"?

"Yup, that same nigga", Mac says as he finishes his beer.

Toni stands up. "I told you I didn't like that nigga fam. On Blood I told you to watch that nigga bro. I told you", he yells as he starts pacing back and forth.

"So what you want to do"? OG asks. "You know it's been a while and I've changed my life up, but I can still pull rank and make some shit pop."

"I think for now I'm going to let it ride, but I'll keep that in mind", Mac says

"See, now that's your problem Mac.. you're too nice."

"What do you mean"? Mac asks.

"Man you always turn the other cheek bro", he says. "This nigga, he violated, broke code and it needs to be dealt with point blank."

"He's right", OG says.

Mac drops his head.

"Look bro. I'm gonna go and holla at this nigga."

Mac then looks up.

"I'm not going to hurt him, I just want to talk", Tony says as he walks out the door.

OG gets up and locks the door. "You know T's right Mac, he says as he grabs a brew. "You lucky you got him as a friend."

Tony pulls up to the gas station. Inside are Mark and his girl Sara.

"Welcome, how can I help you", the cashier asks.

"Yea is Mark here"? Tony asks

"Yes I'm Mark. Do I know you"?

"No, just know that I'm one of Mac's friends."

Mark smiles and turns to his girl. "Hey babe go back home", he says to his girlfriend Sara.

"Sure", she says in a concerned voice. Are you going to be fine?

"Yea", Mark says staring at Tony.

Yeah I'm not going to put my hands on you. Because Mac asked me not to", Tony tells him.

"Yeah, well to be honest it's none of your business", Mark then laughs, "or Mac's either, for that matter."

"Keep being a smart ass and I'll FUCK your ass up my damn self", Tony screams as he points at Mark.

"Get your finger out of my face", Mark says aggressively as he smacks Tony's hand away.

"I was trying to be respectful in front of your girl", Tony says. "But fuck it, since you want to be a dick, I'm just gonna say it.

"You shut your mouth punk." Mark says to Tony as he begins to get flustered.

"Mark what is he talking about"? Sara asks feeling confused.

"Nothing Sara, now GO HOME"!! Mark demands.

"Oh! You don't know. Well let me tell you where your boyfriend was last night Sara", Tony says. He was having an affair with my best friend's wife.

"Are you serious", she asks. She then looks at Mark," so that's why you came home so late last night."

Mark goes to hush Tony but Tony flashes his gun hidden beneath his hoodie, stopping Mark.

"That's a Glock", Tony smiles slowly backs up toward the door.

"Yeah, I'll catch you on the rebound buddy", Mark yells. "Oh, and tell Mac I said hey."

Tony gives him the finger and leaves.

Mark then turns to his girl. "I told you to go home, why didn't you listen."

She glares at him and walks out.

"Babe, Babe", he calls as he watches her walk out the door.

Time Lapse

It's been a few weeks since the incident and Mac and Karren have been doing good, they seem to have put the worst behind them and decided to stick together. One day while Karren was returning from a doctor's visit Mark tries to run her off the road. She goes home and tells Mac and all hell breaks loose. Mac calls up his big homie and tells him what happened.

Karren bursts through the doors.

"MAC, MAC"! She yells as she runs over to the couch and hugs him tight.

"What happened"? Mac asked sounding very concerned.

"I was nearly run off the road", she says to him with tears flowing down her face.

"What"!! Mac yells. "Are you and the baby alright"?

"Yeah, we're good", Karren says assuring him as she wipes her face.

"Phew, thank god", he says as he wipes tears from her face as well. "Calm down you're safe now. When did all this happen"? Mac asks as he opens the door to go and get a look at the car.

"The car is fine", she tells him. "He missed me and that's what caused me to spin out of control."

"So what happened"?

"I was coming back from the doctor's", she tells him. And I was passing an intersection because I had the right of way. So I see this one car sitting at the light and just as I'm about to pass him, he pulls right out in front of me nearly hitting me. If I didn't jerk the wheel then he would've"!

"And after that the car spun out of control"? Mac asks interrupting her. "Did you call the police"?

"That fucker kept going", Karen says to him. "But I was able to get a look at the person, and you're never gonna guess who it was."

Mac pauses. "Don't tell me it was him." He says as he looks her dead in her eyes.

"Yeah, I see him."

"That's it, that nigga is dead", Mac says as he goes inside.

"Mac what are you gonna do"? Karen asks.

"Look, go into the bedroom, get washed up and relax. I'm going to handle this, don't worry about it", Mac says to Karren as he kisses her on her forehead.

Karren gets up and walks into the bedroom. Mac immediately jumps on his phone and gets on Facebook to make a post. "Karren was run off the road but she is safe.... Thank God..." #heisgood.

After posting it people instantly begin to react to the status and comment. Mac then calls OG......

"Aye yo OG, it's Mac", he says.

"What's up lil bro", OG replies. "Yeah, I just saw the crazy shit you just posted. Thank God she and the baby are safe."

"Yeah the almighty is indeed good. But that's not why I'm calling you OG."

"Haha yeah I figured. I guess you couldn't turn the other cheek on this one huh."

"No OG. Wrong book. This time it's an eye for an eye."

"Haha I got you. So are you sure it was him. I just want to be certain before I call the hit baby bro."

"Yeah OG, she said she'd seen the bastard behind the wheel with no one else with him."

"Cool, say less, let's just hope he's all alone this time too, I'm going to text you later"... he says as he hangs up.

Fast forward a few hours, now the time is now 10:30pm.

Mark has gotten home from work and he's inside relaxing and seems to be the only one there. Suddenly a black old school sedan pulls up in front of Mark's house and just sits there. Mark goes to his window to look at the car and notices the car doesn't have any tags. He quickly realizes what's going on and gets away from the window. Suddenly 4 masked gunmen hangout the windows of the 4 door car and begin to open fire upon Mark's car and house. Once done the car peels off. Once the bullets stop Mark gets up and runs outside and begins to shoot at the fleeing car.

It then cuts back to Mac. He just received a text with the stop sign emoji from OG. Mac smiles as he closes his phone and goes into the room with Karren and he closes the door.

The next day Mac gets a text from Mark. It's about ending the beef. Mark apologizes for his actions. He says he knows he was wrong and wanted to know if they were still cool. Mac says yeah. Mark tells him that he was quitting the gas station and going somewhere else.

Weeks later Karren gave birth to a baby boy and they named him Samuel after the biblical prophet.

8

A Chance At Love

by Dayle Duncan

Ashley stared at her computer screen anxiously as she had done every night over the last two months. Although she felt silly she remembered what Diane had told her while she was clipping away at Ashley's damp dark brown hair.

"Honey, you really should take advantage of those dating sites I gave you. There is plenty of love out there you just need to make yourself available, you know? Market yourself while you're still young and beautiful, Baby."

This was months ago and finally Ashley accepted the challenge, secretly of course. Was this the right way? Since her engagement to Shane was called off two years ago she'd been living like a hermit. Despite many blind dates she just could not let herself become vulnerable again. She would not allow herself to be betrayed again. At twenty-four she was happy on her own, working from home as a freelance graphic multimedia designer. She was her own boss but quite single.

"It's perfectly safe." Anna had joined in sweeping the floor in slow steady movements. *"If you don't like the picture, just swipe on."* Giggling she added. *"After all, don't we all just love eye candy?"*

"Okay, Ashley. You can do this." She took a deep breath and signed in. Lovebird. While the icon swirled around she refilled her coffee mug. When she returned she found a few winks and messages, those obscene, deleted. No one really caught her eye until she saw someone new. Todd30. Her heart skipped a beat. A bright cheeky grin lifted his perfectly structured face to dazzling blue eyes. She was hooked; panic stricken and intrigued. She moved the cursor to the green icon. Yes? No? Closing her eyes she clicked; a wink, an invite. She covered her inward excitement with her mouth as if she were going to scream in delight. Her heart raced, she actually did it! Would he reply?

Thirty minutes later she signed off feeling slightly deflated. She wanted to kick herself, why did she do that? Why?

What if he doesn't like her photo or her profile! She chastised herself for thinking she'd get a response immediately and let out a sigh. Four different dating sites and no one responded to her requests or she received outrageous responses.

"Maybe he's busy or just offline." She told Maestro, her kitten curled up in a ball on her lap, stroking him gently as she looked out the window at the still dark night. There were no stars tonight.

She felt close to giving up. Still, she hoped.

The radio station blared through her alarm clock blinking an obnoxious red 05:00. With a groan she began flapping her arm in the air reaching out for the snooze button. With a giant yawn she wiggled from under the covers trying not to disturb Maestro sleeping soundly on top of her stomach. He was worse than her in the mornings. Sometimes he refused to move.

She checked her phone for any notifications from *DateTheOne.com* for that one wink or message from *Todd30* that she desperately wanted to receive, but there was not even a perverse message from an unknown.

The day flew by in a daze. She battled to concentrate on the latest project for a client due at 5PM. Soon it turned into days, then a week, two weeks. Every night only those dazzling blue eyes greeted her and that cheeky smile, she could not resist but to smile back.

"I can't go on another blind date." Ashley fell backwards on her bed in frustration, her hands covering her face. How did she land up with such a bossy sister?

"It has already been arranged." Claire opened Ashley's cupboard and whipped through the clothing. "You can't rely on these dating sites and personally I don't trust them. All the girls agreed on this and we found the perfect guy for you. We'll all meet up at Legend's Sports Bar at 8PM." Somehow Claire had found out about the dating sites.

After a few minutes Claire pulled out a thin strapped short black dress with thin silver sequences along the neckline. "This is perfect!" She exclaimed. Looking at Ashley from top to bottom, she said. "The black shoes I gave you for Christmas, you must wear them."

"How are we even related?" Ashley shifted slightly, leaning on her elbow, watching her elder sister move around the room as if she were designing a new home.

Legend's Sports Bar was not Ashley's favorite place but she enjoyed the atmosphere and the live bands. She felt a little overdressed but there was no arguing with Claire once her mind was made up. It's a wonder how Gary puts up with her. Ashley smiled as she remembered the one time where Claire snuck out the house for one of her friends' brother's eighteenth birthday party. Being thirteen at the time Claire had thought that she was adult enough to go and Ashley had to run between their rooms and pretend as if Claire was sleeping. Claire insisted that it had to look real, not a stuffed doll or pieces of clothing hidden underneath the duvet covers.

"And this is my sister, Ashley." Claire's voice was loud and commanding with Gary, Mary-Jane, Lydia, Thomas and Dane following after her. There were a few newbies in Claire's entourage that Ashley had never met before. She looked at the man Claire introduced as Michael. *No wonder Claire insisted on the uncomfortable high-heeled shoes*, she thought looking up at him with a smile. His dark blond hair was short, combed neatly upwards in the front. Ashley appreciated him dressing up for the occasion in a smart dark blue shirt, white tie and black trousers. He may have played rugby in his younger days. Claire and her entourage disappeared as quickly as they had arrived.

"I like this band." Michael said leaning forward. "My sister is the drummer."

Something about his statement made them both laugh. *Nice icebreaker*, Ashley thought and decided a good response would be to agree with him and compliment the band.

"If it wasn't for my sister I'd probably be home watching Titanic with my cat." Ashley told him with a laugh, taking a sip of her cider. *He has a great smile*, she thought noticing dimples.

Watching his lips move she tried hard to focus on the conversation, his soft voice eager to tell her all about being a stockbroker but that was all she heard - stockbroker.

Nothing like home sweet home, Ashley thought feeling refreshed and ready to tackle the world. Perhaps Claire was right. Maybe -

Her phone rang breaking her deep thoughts. It was Claire.

"Tell me everything!"

"Nothing to tell really, he was really nice though."

"Oh, god. No, Ashley! I could tell he's really into you. When are you going to see him again?"

"Um, I don't know but he may call sometime."

"What am I going to do with you?" Ashley could almost hear Claire rolling her eyes with a frustrated sigh. "I worry a lot about you? My heart broke when Shane cheated on you. Give Michael a chance, okay?"

"Okay, okay." Ashley knew her sister would not give up. "If he calls I'll go out with him again."

Finally satisfied Claire ended the call.

Maestro began clawing Ashley's leg as if it were a tree. His tiny claws were like knives. *Damn*, she forgot to feed him earlier before she left with Claire. As she dished up his food she heard a loud ping come from her computer. Her heart raced. *Was it?*

Leaving the cat bowl on the kitchen counter for an irritated Maestro to figure out how to get to his meal, she rushed over to the computer. *It was!*

It was not those dazzling blue eyes and cheeky smile that greeted her. In unread green was a message from Todd30. Ashley suddenly felt hot and cold and thought she'd faint. Telling herself to calm down she opened the message.

Todd30: "Hi, I am sorry to get back to you after such a long time I have been out the country. How are you?"

He was still online! What should she say? What would Claire say? Okay, she was not Claire.

Lovebird: "Hi, I am fine thank you. I have also been quite busy so it's alright, I understand."

Todd30: "I really like your profile."

Ashley's phone rang. It was Michael. Feeling slightly guilty she let the call go to voicemail.

Todd30: "I am quite a simple person. My profile pretty much explains who I am. My name is Todd. I guess my login name gives it away – smiley face."

Lovebird: "My name is Ashley."

Ashley felt like she was floating in the sky, above the soft clouds bathing in sunlight as she and Todd chatted almost all night. Lying in bed with Maestro across her chest, Ashley closed her eyes and dreamt of Todd, the man with the cheeky grin and dazzling blue eyes.

Claire was horrified and defiant. "How could you do that? I had to make up a lie for you, that you passed out or something and didn't hear your phone ringing."

Ashley balanced her phone in the crook of her neck as she replied to Todd's messages he'd sent after she'd logged off last night. She barely heard her sister's screaming.

"Yeah. Sure." Ashley said absentmindedly, typing away. *Todd wanted to meet!*

"Ashley, are you even listening?" A sigh. "He is willing to meet you again on Saturday night-"

"No can do, Claire." Ashley felt invincible standing up to her sister.

"What? Why?"

"Because I am going to meet Todd."

"Todd? Who's that?"

"Dazzling," Ashley said softly and ended the call.

Ashley ignored Claire's thirty-five calls and twenty-nine messages over the course of the week. She'd explain later and Claire would forgive her. Right now she needed to think straight. She felt bad about Michael, but at the same time felt great about

Todd. When she spoke to Diane again of her view on online dating she had changed her mind and was grumpy about it.

"She met someone who wasn't real." Anna whispered in Ashley's ear.

What if Todd wasn't real? What if he didn't come and meet her? Maybe Claire was right and she should rather give Michael a chance.

"He will be waiting for you." Ashley listened to Claire's messages. "Harlequins at 7PM."

She arranged to meet Todd at the Moses Mabhida Stadium. For a moment she felt conflicted. What if she experienced the same disappointment as Diane?

"What should I do, Maestro?" Ashley said sadly. "I'm scared I will make the wrong choice."

The kitten stared, listening as if provided with all the answers and suddenly attacked Ashley's sock cladded feet.

Saturday slowly arrived. Ashley knew what she should do and it would change the course of her life forever. It was inevitable that someone would be hurt but she couldn't stop that from happening. The drive was not long and reached her destination early. Taking a deep breath she walked towards the building avoiding the small crowds of people. The sky arc shone underneath the sunset. Time ticked and she became nervous, anxious. She looked around. *Where was he?*

Suddenly the sky exploded with the whirring sound of a helicopter. Gathered crowds dissipated as the helicopter began its landing. From the helicopter a loud hailer sounded calling *her name!*

Walking towards the helicopter a man came out. Ashley froze as she realised this person was walking towards her.

"You are far more beautiful in person." He said with a slight accent and smiled. "Helicopter is a bit over the top but I didn't want to be late."

Mesmerised, she said nothing and let him take her hand and lead her to the helicopter.

As Ashley found her small leap of faith that gave her the chance of love; so did Michael when he met a lovely woman at Harlequin's Bar.

9

Love In Paro's Time

by Khyati Bali

I came back from college with swollen eyes and went straight into my room. After a few minutes I had a knock at my door. It was Paro, my grandmother and in her very sweet voice she said, "Aaina you can always share it out." With a very quivering voice I asked her, "If I let you in will you give me a bear hug".

'Bear hug' is a short form that I gave to those long hugs where you just forget whatever else is happening around you for a minute. Paro and I are more like best friends. I call her Paro because it's her favorite Bollywood movie character's name. She came into my room and gave me a big bear hug. And then she asked me, "what made you cry so bad that too in college?"

I gathered all my courage and told her that Ishan, the guy I had been dating for the past 8 months was still using the online app we met through for hook ups and had been cheating on me. After a moment of awkward silence she asked me, "so the jerk who had been picking you up on the weekends for the past few months, his name is Ishan?" I was a bit astonished to hear her call him a jerk. "What, he looks like a jerk to you?" The girlfriend in me got a little offended but then I was hit by a wave of sadness, it reminded me about the hurt he had caused me and the way he had ditched me.

Tears started rolling down my checks and I started sobbing in Paro's lap. She very politely said, "I thought maybe it's just his looks but after what he has done to you he is definitely a one! Stop crying Aaina, my love you are stronger than you think."

She wiped my tears, gave me a glass of water and asked me to take some deep breaths. "Well I know you are hurt right now but I'm also a little mad at you." "Wait, what are you mad at me about?" "You call me your best friend don't you?" "Of course I do. What about it?" "Then tell me why am I getting to know that you were dating someone after your breakup?"

I was left speechless for a while and then I began to cotton on what exactly Paro was trying to ask. She had always been there for me whether it was some stupid science project or me having a fight with my parents or on the days when I would fall sick, she would stay by my side all day long and even during my exams she would stay up with me. But ever since I got in college I was caught up in myself so much that I hardly gave time to Paro and still she's here when I need here the most. I took her hand and held it, conscience stricken and said," I'm really sorry for being so thoughtless." "There's no need to say sorry, I'm glad at least you were able to acknowledge it. Anyways, do you mind telling me where did you meet this Ishan"? "Everybody in my gang at college was dating someone. They wanted me to date as well. At first they started setting me up with someone they knew but it wasn't working for me. I just couldn't vibe with any of the guys I met." "So you wanted to date someone because your friends wanted you to? Not because you wanted to??" Paro was aghast at what I had just told her.

"Yes but this wasn't the only reason you know. I used to feel lonely every time I saw people going on movie dates, long drives after college and what not. I started doubting myself so one night I downloaded this online dating app and that's where I saw Ishan's profile. He looked nice and had a very funny bio so I swiped right and we started talking. After 3 weeks of talking he asked me out for a date. He made our first date really special. That evening when he dropped me home I knew he was the one but I didn't know that one day he would cheat on me and leave me like I never meant anything to him." "So how did you find out that he was cheating on you?" "I started feeling ignored, he was never like that before but now he would cancel our plans. I tried asking him but he said that he was busy and a little stressed out about the exams. I thought maybe he needed a little space and to me that was completely fine.

But today while we were sitting in our college's canteen, Ishan and his friend went to washroom and Ishan forgot to take his phone with him. It started buzzing so I picked it up. There were messages on the same online dating app from some girl named Tanya. I opened the chat and found out that they were together since last two months. I couldn't believe my eyes. And I still don't know what I did to deserve all of this." I again burst into tears after telling this to Paro. With a broken heart I ask her, "Why is it so hard to find true love these days Paro?" She smiled and said, "do you know that I met your grandfather for the very first time on our wedding day?" "No way! How could you marry someone just like that?" It sounded so daunting to me, marrying someone who doesn't even know what you looked like. "I see this generation swiping right to find love but back in our time we could only hope to find love in the man we were destined to marry. You see, we didn't have these many options."

"Paro, did you fall in love with grandpa or did you just settle?" I was so curious to know about how Paro had fallen for grandpa that for a moment my heart stopped aching.

"Well he was a dashing man with bushy moustache and looked quite charming to me. But I didn't know what kind of person he was. You see, I was 21 years old and I was being married in a family that had a well settled business. That's all I knew about them. I was sad because I had to leave my parents, I was so nervous about how my life would completely change after that day. The matters of heart Aaina, they need time, space, trust and patience to evolve into something heavenly. And your grandpa and I gave it all. It wasn't easy at first, we were two different humans with different opinions and we were complete strangers. After our marriage we only wished each other good morning and good night for the first ten days. Our home was filled with guests and we could barely see each other but whenever we would get a glimpse of one another we would pass a smile. Then slowly we started to know each other. I learned to make his favorite dishes and he would bring me my favorite flowers while returning home from work. After a year we had our first child, your father. During the last month of my pregnancy your grandpa stopped going to work so that he could take care of me. His family wasn't supportive towards his decision but he didn't listen to them and provided me every comfort he could.

Time passed and after few years we were blessed with our second child, your paternal aunt. But soon after her birth your grandpa had to leave for America for some business tour. It was a big decision but I supported him and asked him not to worry about his family and promised him that I would take care of everyone. He had gone for a year. I would hear our neighbours talk like "oh, she thinks her husband would not cheat on her. Everybody knows what men do when they are away from home" every time I took a stroll to the nearby market. I would cry on my way back to home.

But I never doubted your grandpa. We would write each other letters telling everything that's been happening and expressing everything we felt. When I went to receive him at the airport he came running towards me the moment he saw me. We hugged each other for so long. And that day we realized how much we truly loved each other." "THAT'S SO CUTE PARO!!!! It's like you and grandpa lived the perfect love story." "We had our ups and downs but we made our way through life because we never gave up on each other."

"Paro if you and grandpa could fall for each other that too in an arrange marriage then why do so many people who do love marriages are knocking the doors of courts to get a divorce these days?" "This generation is very aware of what's right and wrong no offense to that, but somewhere I think your generation expects too much in the name of love and forgets that it's okay if love isn't extraordinary on all days because love being it's best version only needs to be." Paro had said that with so much ease and everything that she said was so true. Maybe it's not love that's baffling, maybe it's the new generation, us.

10

Don't Let It Slip

by Lily Nielsen

The beat of your heart is technically caused by your body's urge to live. You yourself are not telling your heart to swell up with blood to the point where it's about to burst. We have no control over how fast it's going, or how much blood it's pumping in each beat. As kids, we probably all tried to control it, but in the end we were unsuccessful. I'm not sure why that is. But I still wish that I could.

My body moves at a pace, just like everybody else's does. To some, it might be to the beat of their favorite song, or the ticking of a clock. But mine moves to the beat of my heart. How I despise the beat of my heart.

No one goes looking for danger, but sometimes the speed of your heart just forces you to face your fears. And when your body follows your already too-fast heart rate, you start to wish that you could slow it down and run away from the danger.

I arrived at the coffee shop five minutes early. Thanks to my fast feet. But he was early too, and that just made me want to barf.

"Effie, hey." I heard him call just as I stepped inside.

I looked up and accidentally made eye contact with the boy who gave me butterflies. I'm not sure how long I ended up staring at him, but it was long enough for him to avert his own gaze and look down to the floor.

I was tempted to walk over to him, and it might have been some mark of my feminist agenda or something, but I decided against feminism for the day and chose to stay right where I was, waiting for the boy to make the first move.

It took him a moment, but he finally realized that I was waiting for him to approach, and so he walked over. "You look good," he told me, gesturing to my cheap overalls. "Well Thank you," I replied, "You too." He didn't have to know that I got them on sale.

I suddenly became aware that my heart was beating loudly. Louder than a metronome, it was thumping louder and faster than I would have ever wanted. I needed something, anything to distract me from the noise, or the sweat stains hiding under my armpits. I needed- "Do you want to order something?" I let out a sigh of relief, thankful that he turned the conversation himself. "Yes," I exhaled, trying to collect my nerves before I made a fool of myself.

A skinny barista with purple hair was the first to answer to our beacon of assistance. Maddie, as her name tag suggested. "Could I have an espresso con panna?" he asked. Hearing this, a sickly feeling fell over me. I stalked his Instagram. I know, it doesn't sound too bad. And really, it's not, everybody does it. But the problem was that I also stalked his Facebook, Twitter, LinkedIn and followed his location on Snapchat.

I wish I could say that it was his fault. After all, he was the one who'd left the map on. But secretly, I knew it was my fault. I'm a creep! According to his Instagram, espresso con panna was his "favorite drink", and his first taste of it was during a trip to Italy three years ago. That was a piece of information that I shouldn't have known, which meant that I was a stalker.

A sense of panic started to come over me, that maybe I had dug a bit too far into his personal life. I knew it was almost definite that I accidentally let something slip and he'd know that I was a creep whom he most certainly didn't want to date.

"And you?" The barista asked me, "What would you like?"

My normal order was simple: Green tea. But then I was reminded of something, "China" that was where green tea came from and he'd been to China on his travels before. What if he knew I'd been stalking him because of that random coincidence? I couldn't risk that. All of the words in my brain started to mix up and turn into slop, I couldn't form sounds and it all just came out in a mumbled gush. "Coffee?" I replied.

The barista raised her eyebrows at me, "What kind of coffee?" she asked me, "Just black coffee?" I couldn't think of a reply soon enough. I was panicking and needed help, but my stupid self wouldn't allow it. "Yes?" I replied, but soon rushed to correct myself so that I sounded positive of my answer, "Yes. Yes, I would like plain coffee." She gave a judgmental look, but allowed my boring drink choice to slide as she picked up a marker. "Name?"

"Effie," I responded.

There was only one table available, hiding in the back corner of the coffee shop. We made our way over to it, drinks in hand and an inclined mental breakdown preparing itself. "It's so nice outside," he said. I simply nodded my head, my mind switching randomly to how he spent his summer in the even nicer heat.

"Well I'm sure you've seen nicer," I spat out, quickly regretting it and wanting to take back everything I've ever done.

He chuckled and took a sip of coffee, coaxing me to do the same.

Now, according to a post that he "re-tweeted", he loves coffee. And according to my taste buds, coffee tastes like bitter, hot dirt was scooped into a mug, slushed around for a few minutes and served like it was the best thing since sliced bread. But he did think it was the best thing since sliced bread. A coffee lover and a tea drinker are not a perfect match. Could you imagine the daily debate that would cause? So I needed to pretend, I needed to act. Yes! I was an actor, the best one in Hollywood and I loved coffee!

I leaned back in my chair, acting cool as the coffee lover that I was supposed to be. "How's your drink?" I asked him.

He took another sip nodding his head as it travelled down his throat. "Good," he replied. "You know, the first time I tried one of these, I was in Italy."

Actually, I knew that, but it's not like I could say anything about it. "Really?"

"Yeah, I'm quite a traveller."

"Which was your favorite place to go?"

"Definitely a cruise in the Bermuda Triangle."

I nearly spit out my drink, "I thought it was New Zealand."

He started eyeing me, probably wondering how I knew he'd been there. I turned a sheepish shade of red and downed some disgusting coffee, just to keep myself busy. "How did you know that I've been to New Zealand?"

"A wild guess!" Which was a lie, but sometimes, especially in cases where your date is about to file a restraining order, you have to lie.

"Well either way, it was the Bermuda Triangle. It was really cool too, I was really nervous, especially because there are so many stories of cruise ships sinking there, but I survived." He droned on and on about his fascination with unsolved mysteries, not like I wouldn't know any of those thoughts. He was a big watcher of The History Channel.

"So where else have you been?" I asked, starting to tick locations off of my fingers, anything to get the hot mug out of my hand. "China, Greece, India, London, Hawaii?"

His eyebrows raised, and I realized what I had done. Holy crap. He knew. "Actually all of those places."

His mouth moved open to speak, my cue to leave so that I didn't cause more damage. He reached out quickly though, stopping me, "Hey are you okay?"

They say that you can't lie to somebody that you have a crush on, which is true, you can't. I had been trying to keep all of this information that I so wrongly knew to myself, but now it was bubbling up inside of me, and I needed somebody to throw up on. Unfortunately, he was the closest. I had no choice.

"I stalked you!"

He raised his eyebrows slightly and looked down at me. "You did?"

"I did and I'm so sorry, I shouldn't have, I just really wanted to get to know you better before this train wreck of a date and so I looked you up and I just took it a bit too far, and-"

"Effie," he said, cutting me off quickly. "It's okay. I stalked you too."

"You did?"

"Everybody stalks people on the internet. You're fine."

Oh. Everybody stalks people on the internet. Good to know. But now I looked stupid.

People were staring at me, a girl who's just had a mental breakdown in the middle of a coffee shop ruining her date. "I'm sorry," I whispered.

"It's okay," he whispered back.

The two of us stood up, unanimously deciding to leave the cafe. We walked outside, drinks in our hands and took off down the street. It made me feel better that he'd stalked me too, but it still wasn't okay of me to know all of that uncomfortable information. "Oh wait!" He called running back into the shop and leaving me stranded.

He came back a few minutes later with another steaming drink in his hand. "According to your Instagram story, you hate coffee."

I took the cup from him, taking in a sniff of the earthy green tea. "China's best."

And so we walked and talked, laughing about the funny things we'd learned about the other. And this time it was to the pace of my calm heart.

11

Modern Love – Hook Ups Or Romance?

by Munmun Aidasani

From stolen looks across bookshelves in the library to conversation over coffee to right swipe on Tinder, dating has come a long way. Thanks to smartphones and the internet our options are unlimited, whether it's a retail item or a romantic possibility. We all have become maximizers. Living alone can be liberating, maddening, joyful, or lonely. The old-fashioned version of courting was what our parents or we experienced but our new generation wants it all, without the excess baggage of commitment.

The culture of online dating before marriage is trendy nowadays. Dating can be a magical way to decode your spouse. People start dating and try to reveal unknown things, likes, dislikes, etc. Dating brings excitement. It brings newness.

Lisa, a friend and a dating expert asked Asha to find her match online. Although Asha was not interested, it's not like that she was against online dating for other people. It's just she didn't want her story to be "We met on match.com".

She always thought online match making as a waste of both time and money, but there was ever growing sense of existential dread rising up day by day, convincing her that she was probably going to die alone. So, she joined various online matchmaking sites and resigned herself to this experiment.

For more than 3 weeks she had a lot of quantity, but little quality in the candidates coming her way. It was like browsing a book store, except instead of finding a whole stack of new favourites, she was leaving empty handed.

Less than a week later, she got a message from Abhay saying – "Hello" and so as the conversation started.

Abhay and Asha were not sure where to start, and after few days of late-night phone calls and texting, they just fixed the date for watching a movie. After the movie they talked until dusk and looped around the park trails for hours.

Abhay began listing his hesitations about relationships.

"I am working through a breakup,"- he said. Well it ended a year ago, but I am not sure if I am grounded.

After a long pause, he asked Asha's experience about relationships, she was not sure what to say, so she pointed out that it was getting late and that he should drop her home.

Before leaving, he said, he had never met anyone who looked like Asha and asked for their next date.

On their second date, they sat down at a café for breakfast. After some chit-chat, Abhay told Asha that he has some urgent business meeting so has to leave early.

Asha just smiled and took her bag, Abhay tried to come closer, she dodged his kiss and gave him a peck on the cheek instead. On her way home she got a text asking if she was sure, she doesn't want a kiss?

Asha replied, “Abhay, honestly things are moving a little too fast for my liking and I am not ready as yet.”

Asha took her time and after enough pondering over Abahy on their next dinner date, Asha said, “Abhay, you closely fit my heart, I was looking for someone intelligent, down to earth, and one who can keep up with my sense of humour, and I can see all these qualities in you.

“What” he asked, twitching awake.

I feel love for you.”- said Asha.

“Really?”- said Abhay.

When they got back into his car, Abhay said, “I guess there are a few things we should talk about.”

Look Asha, you should be very clear, I just want some sort of fun and excitement I don’t believe in long term relationships. I just wanted the refreshing sleep overs with you.

Asha instantly got creeper vibes and was like “No”.

You mean to say Abhay, that to find my prince, I have to kiss a few frogs along the way?

“When was the last time you had sex”? Abhay asked.

“Abhay, that’s incredibly inappropriate. I am still a virgin. I cannot lose my virginity for any random man.”- said Asha.

She was not sure if he heard her clearly.

What? You are still a virgin, then what are you doing on this dating app? Are you ready for a casual hookup? -asked Abhay.

“I just wanted to decode my suitable partner; I did not know that this ends in hook ups. I am not here to do kinky shit” –Asha said in an angry tone.

It was another couple of hours, before he realized she was breaking up with him. It was a 5 hour long conversation from his car to sitting lakeside near Asha's house and she could make sense of the down fall and just figured out that they would never see each other again. Things immediately took a turn for the worst. And finally, she announced the breakup, blankly at one point once they were back in the car, staring out of the window.

"Don't chase a man who doesn't want you, and who doesn't respect your feelings", she told herself and got out of the car without looking back.

She regrets that she spent so many days conversing with him on text messages and calls and then ended up things in such an unexpected way. How did I believe him, that he could be my right choice, for him dating was just a game? I was clingy and desperate and wore my heart on sleeve, fell madly in love with him just to meet heartbreaking rejection from him.

I don't perceive that this generation can ever fathom what real romance/love is. To me, Romance is a way of life. It's not a one-day affair but a lifetime of adulation. Once you decide on the man or woman you want to stand by there begins the first step of desire. Romance is a slow seductive passion that gently weaves its way around you. It's the happiness that you exude when you are together and it's the calm serenity you feel when you are apart.

Modern love or relationships does not portray surrendering oneself for your love or compromising with everything and sulk to stay in the wed-lock.

Real-life relations are being replaced by digital space. Gone are the days when romance meant "Hallmarked cards and mesmerizing eye contact on dinner dates". People have migrated from selfish to cell fish. In place of expectation, textpectation has become a major concern. The alacrity with which relationships have become deceitful is cumulative. Real and pure love has been lost in this labyrinth. Welcome to the new age romance. It's not about love, it's about the spur of the moment, it's about the chase and it's about the casualness of sex.

People are getting bored of long-lasting relations. They are overwhelmed with the new era of online dating and are bored with their monotonous life; such online apps are becoming a lifeline for such people.

The unfortunate coincidence is that the fine-tuned analysis of the dating numbers game and streamlining of its trial and error process of shopping around have taken place. As dating's definitions has expanded from the search for a suitable marriage partner into something decidedly more ambiguous. The winding road from the classified section of you to Tinder, Bumble etc. has taken an unexpected turn. It's easy to see why online dating has taken off. It provides you with a seemingly endless supply of people who are single and looking to date.

Dating is a game of probabilities or ratios or a marketplace in which a single person just has to keep shopping until he/she finds 'the one'. The minute either partner gets too close for comfort and uses the dreaded word "love" or "miss"; they want to run the other direction as fast as their legs can carry them. Yes, they like each other and enjoy the time they spend together. They hook up, have sex.... go on holidays, live life truly king size. But that's it ... they are not willing to go beyond. Dating apps have rapidly become the mode du jour for single people to meet each other, have sex and romance even more like shopping.

It's true more and more people are finding real and lasting relationships online but, in my life, I experienced an awkward encounter. It's like you can find 1000 perfect matches from a casted net of 100000 Mr. Wrongs and Ms. Terribles.

12

Awkward Meeting

by Violet Evergarden

"Amy, did you see it?" Lisa nudges my arm with hers while urging me to look in the same direction as hers.

"Lisa, I'm texting and see! Typos!" I groaned a little before correcting the word on my text and I looked up as she pressed me to look. There's a new café that recently opened in our small town. I got to know about it from my brother, who frequently goes there to study. Ha! Like I believe his word of 'studying.'

"It's just a café, Lisa," I commented before I move my eyes to the new notification on my phone. We were still walking side by side even though I ignored where I walked. I know my friend Lisa here would not let me crash on anything on our way. She would frequently pull my arm when I wasn't paying attention and once I almost hit a lamp post.

"Ugh, you ignored what I was trying to show you! There! Look at the notice board near the entrance!" She turns my face to look in the café's direction again. This time, I squinted my eyes before I read the sentence on the chalkboard there.

"Free drink if you sign up with our app and join the crowd! Join us today and get your free drink every day! – Summer Love Café~.'

"Come on! I want to scan their QR code and get a free drink!" Lisa already pushed the traffic light button for us to cross the road and went there. Without much thinking, I came after her and scanned the app as well. As I signed in, someone who just walked out of the café stunned me with his looks. He's godly handsome! I unconsciously gaped open my mouth, and the man looked at me before he smiled and walked away with his venti size cup in his hand.

"Ahem, I know you were shocked, but... it's starting to get hot in here. And he's long gone, Amy." Lisa tapped on my shoulder, and I quickly returned to earth. Wait, he is long gone? So, Lisa saw him too??

"Lisa-"

"Nah-uh, I don't know him, darl. Let's just get our free drinks and return home. I'm tired and need my energy drink right away." She went inside and I quickly finished signing in, I noticed that the app's layout was relatively modern and cute. There are already hundreds of people registering with their app. I complement the management team for their marketing strategy to attract more people to come and increase their sales.

Ding!

A new notice arrived and I saw the invite on the screen. That's a cat photo in the display pic. I frowned a bit when I saw the app trying to mix and match our preference to someone who had similar tastes. And the invitation is only for casual discussion among the members. I accept the invitation and look forward to a drink.

'Did you sign up for our app, miss?' The bartender asks when it is my turn. As I went to open the application and show it to the bartender, a new notification appears one more time.

Ding!

I don't know what's on the screen, but the barmaid in front of me smiles at me before she asks me what kind of drink I want for free. She showed me a list of free drinks before I made my choice.

"Enjoy your drink, Miss. Oh, by the way, the guy is cute." She winks at me before I give her an odd smile. Not knowing what to say, I politely said, "Thank you..."

I turn to my dear friend, Lisa, who is already waiting at the door with half of her drink gone. She was thirsty, I guess. "What's up?"

"Nothing." I shake my head and go back to my phone. Yeah, as the bargirl girl said earlier; the guy is cute, because he uses a cat as his profile picture. He sends me a private DM saying that he would like to be friends with me. Oh well, why not? I'm still single and available. It won't hurt me to be friends with someone cute.

"Happy, aren't you? Did you still imagine the guy earlier?" Lisa teases me. She knows that I would never get a guy like that. He's out of my league! I reply with a scoff. "Like it would ever happen!"

***

A few weeks passed, and I was still texting with this guy I got to know from the Summer Love Café app. His name is Jamie, he's 21 years old which is the same age as me, but different school and living in a different town too. He said he is visiting his aunt who lives here and that's how he ended up signing up for the app.

Ding! A new message pops on my screen and I hurriedly open it. The text is from Jamie.

'I have a surprise for you.'

'A surprise for me?'

I giggled and blushed at the same time. I wonder if he knows that I've started to like him since we started talking a few weeks ago.

'Are you free this evening?'

'Kinda. I have to check on my schedule.'

'Please.'

'Uhm...Yeah, I'm free.'

'Cool. I'll pick you up around 7 o'clock?'

'Do you know where I live?'

"Err...No. You never disclosed where you live or how you look too.'

He's right. I never said a word about myself. But somehow, I am falling for someone just by texting on an app. Is that even possible? I need to know how he's gonna react when he sees me? What's he going to think about me then?

'Hmm, I don't even know how you look!'

'How about you tell me something about you so that I can recognize you immediately?'

'Sounds good. We can meet up at some place, you can pick me up there.'

'Are you sure?'

'Yes.'

'Summer Love Café. At 7 pm. I'll be waiting for you.'

'Lovely. I'll wear a turtleneck shirt and I have a ponytail! You have to guess which one is me.'

'No problem, Missy.'

I giggle once more before I stare at his profile picture. Cute. That's the only word I can come up with.

Ding!

A new message floats back onto my phone's screen, but it's from Lisa. She is asking me out for a drink with other girls in Summer Love Café. Looking at the time right now, I thought why not? I want a free drink for today since I haven't gone there for a while now. And it's still early before our first meeting or date, at the same place.

I reply to Lisa with an OK and quickly dress up. I choose a white turtleneck blouse with a brown high-waist skirt. I fixed my bang a little before I took my bag lying on the bed and shove my phone in it. I ran downstairs and found that my brother was still at home, ready for his part-time shift.

"Going out?" He asked.

"Yeah, Summer Love Café. See ya!"

"Be careful on the road!"

This is how we communicate daily. I don't see him until dawn and late at night. He usually has a class or sometimes he will be at the café, yeah, he's working there now as a part-time bartender.

I look at the sky before I sigh. 'It's going to rain today.' I sped up my pace and once I saw the café, I hurriedly extended my hand, wanting to hold the handle, but before I could reach it, someone from the other direction already pushed it and the door hit my face hard!

"Ouch!" I cried out and held my face with my palm. Seriously, it hurt like hell!

"Oh, sorry! I didn't notice-"

"Ugh, fuck!" I cursed and felt that he was surprised by what I said. I didn't say it to him, I just hate the fact that Lisa and the girls will probably be laughing at me, seeing my face with a red stamp on it.

"I'm sorry." He said again and went inside the café. I didn't manage to look at the man's face as I was busy fishing out my phone from my bag and went inside the café. Right behind that guy earlier.

From behind, I could feel his fresh ocean scent. Refreshing. I realize that I am actually shorter, I had to look up a bit just to see his head. Hmm, nothing weird, just his sexy faux hawk haircut that attracts my attention a bit.

"Welcome Sir, have you signed up-" the bartender greets him; I shift my eyes to the inside of the café, looking for Lisa and the girls. And after a few seconds, I saw them sitting by the corner of the shop, beckoning with a wide smile. I lift my hand, which is still holding my phone, and wave them back.

"Welcome miss-"

I hurriedly turn my body around and walk forward without realizing that the guy in front of me is also turning his body around with a tray of his espresso and a plate of doughnut.

Prang!

"Oh, not again." I sighed deeply when I looked at my white shirt. It is now splashed with black, espresso but luckily, it wasn't hot. My phone was thrown to the floor along with the tray and his doughnut.

"I'm sorry," The guy once again apologizes and bends down to the floor. He tries to pick up my phone and I also bend down, picking up his phone I guess, which is near my heels. "Not your fault, I guess today is a bad day for me," I muttered, a bit sadly.

As I reached for his phone, I saw the screen which was turned on and I unconsciously read the text on his phone before I scrunched my eyebrow a bit. He also turned silent when he reached for my phone.

We both looked at each other before tilting our head a bit and we exchanged our phone back.

"Jamie?"

"Amy?"

I think I drain my blood when I realize that the guy in front of me is the guy I first met a couple of weeks ago! I was in awe of him that day! Oh my god! Oh no! No, no, no... I feel like I wanted the ground to swallow me, what have I done??? I just ruined my image in front of him at our first meeting.

I froze, not knowing what to say, but he suddenly chuckled and went to the counter again. A few seconds later, he came up to me again and handed me a napkin. "Hi Miss Amy, I'm truly sorry for what happened today. As an apology, I would like to invite you for a drink with me?"

I pressed my lips together before my eyes caught Lisa and other girls already cheering for me at the corner of the shop. I smile and nod my head slowly. "Well, I'm drenched in your espresso now."

We laugh at it and the bartender suddenly rings the bell at the counter. "Free drink from Summer Love Café, Miss and Mister."

Both of us turn our heads to the girl and she lifts, two cups of new drinks for us. I blushed even more. I feel like all eyes in the café are now on us. "Coffee?" He softly whispered to me, and replied with "Yes, I would love to."

He took the cup and fished for something inside his pocket before he extended his hand to me. I guess we both were surprised with what just happened. He smiles and I feel like melting seeing it.

I open my palm and he put a white gold heart-shape keychain in my hands before he flips the keychain to another side. I saw the 3 words engraved there, *'I love you.'* And I unconsciously nodded my head before I whispered to him, "Me too."

13

My Wish For You

by Violet Evergarden

Thud!

"Sorry," Says the man holding two cups of coffee in his hands. He was in a hurry to leave the coffee shop.

"It's okay," Vanessa replied and nodded her head a little before she went inside the café. She then lifts up her chin and stares at the menu board behind the counter before the barista greets her a good morning. "Morning miss, have you signed up for our new app? If you sign up for the app and show it to us, we will offer you a free beverage from this list. One cup each day".

Vanessa nods her head again while listening to the barista who explains the app to her. Without thinking much, she downloads the app and registers in their system before she starts ordering her Frappuccino and goes to find a seat in the café. As she enjoys her drink, a pair of eyes keep staring at her from afar.

"Aiden!" A group of three people went to the young man who was having his morning breakfast before going to the university. He nearly chokes when one of them patted on his shoulder, before he shot a glare at the three of them. "What the hell man."

"Hehe" one of them chuckles as he got hold of a seat beside Aiden and looked round them for a second, "What'cha looking at?" He asked, seeing nothing which might attract this playboy to get lost in thought.

"A gem," Aiden replied shortly before he took his bag and hit it gently on his friend's head. "Let's move. Professor Dan is probably looking for us at the moment, "he pulled out his cell phone, typing something before a little curve appeared on his face.

Ding!

Vanessa turned her head toward the phone on the table before looking around. A message from somebody called Aiden caught her attention. She doesn't know anyone by the name of Aiden except the one who is the king of Casanova in her faculty. This is definitely a different Aiden, because that Aiden will never look at a woman like her.

She is a gloomy person; she doesn't have too many friends and is mostly alone. She didn't talk to other people too. She is constantly wearing her mask that covers half of her face and the rest with her round glasses. She often wears a cap to cover her hair, which is not in the best condition and sometimes she would wear a wig and cover it with a hat, like today.

Sliding open the text, she read it, *'Hi, beautiful,'* rolling her eyes, she ignores the text and continues to enjoy sightseeing the view from outside the café. It looks like it's going to rain today. As she was absorbed in her own world, another text came in. *'Try their strawberry pie. It's the best in town,'*

Lifting up her eyebrow after seeing the text, Vanessa replied with a simple word, *'Thanks. But not a fan of sweet desserts,'* Yeah, she likes it, but it was restricted in her diet, so, no sweet food for her.

Ding! Another text came in from the same person yet again. *'Me neither. However, I heard from my friend they have the best in town. By the way, Missy, I'm Aiden. What's your name?'*

'Not interested,'

'Oh, that's quite a rare name. Rather, I found it very interesting,'

'Stop sending me messages,'

'Wait! Actually, I want to be friends with you?'

'No, I don't want to,'

'Aww~ but why? It won't harm both of us anyway,'

Vanessa sighed a bit. Yeah, what the guy said is true. It won't harm both of them if they befriend each other. However, with her condition, would it be okay to have friends? She never had one before, no, actually in her entire life. She was always alone.

'What is your intention?'

'Hm? To be your friend.'

'If I refuse?'

'I'll try until you say yes,'

'Why are you so eager to be friends with me?'

'Why are you so eager to reject it anyway?'

'Ugh,'

'Ahaha, come on~ say yes,'

'No,'

'Please,'

'I don't know you, weirdo,'

'Eh? Aren't I already telling you my name? It's Aiden. You can call me Ai, which means 'love'. You can also call me Aid, I'll come right away and save your day, Missy,'

Vanessa chuckles as she reads the last two sentences. This guy is persistent and she found it cute. Well, how does it feel like to have a friend? Maybe.... just maybe this could make her at least happy in her remaining days here? She thought of why not just trying her luck and wish that everything will go okay.

'I'm Vanessa,' she replied to the guy and the ticking sound of the glass window beside her makes her realize that it's already raining outside. She finishes her Frappuccino and grabs her coat hung on the chair beside her before she ran back to her house.

***

"You look happy!" Aiden's friend glances at him as he continues to smile and sometimes, he would chuckle while reading the text on his phone. It makes him wonder, why he reacts like he was struck by the love bug these few days.

"Yeah, I'm in love," Aiden replied without looking at his friend. Since a few days he has been constantly chatting with a girl named Vanessa. He hasn't seen her in the faculty recently but he does remember that he once saw her during the beginning of the semester. She's different from other girls and he found her interesting and easy to talk to, leaving aside her odd behaviour sometimes.

As the day is almost over, Aiden suddenly remembers that he still needs to give his report to the professor before the day ends. He took a shortcut to the professors' room by passing down the music hall. However, as soon as he walks outside the hall, he can hear someone playing the piano in the hall.

It is a piece of Yiruma's song, Kiss the Rain, however, the music that is playing right now sounds so sad... like all hope is gone. He stays behind the wall and enjoys the music until it finishes and he then runs back to the professor's room.

Inside the hall, Vanessa wiped her tears while staring at the piano before she stood up and left the hall. Today, she received a bad news that made her want to play the sad song and vent out all of her feelings into it.

Once she reached her house, she slumped on the floor and started sobbing thinking of her life that will end in just a few days. Earlier, she was okay and accepted her fate. She knew that sooner or later; she will have to go. However, after knowing it was this soon, she didn't think she was ready for it.

Slowly, she took out her phone and typed something and hastily hit send.

'Aiden, will you accompany me for a day trip?'

Aiden who was also returning home smiled reading the text he got from the girl he had a crush on. He immediately replies with, 'Sure. This weekend?'

'Yeah. We'll meet up at the café?'

'Sure!'

***

The day they decide to meet comes and Vanessa tries her best to look very beautiful for Aiden. She wore a little makeup to hide her pale skin and wore a velvety red lipstick with a long wig with straight hair. She didn't wear her mask as she used to, but instead, she went all out with her appearance for today's trip. She looked gorgeous.

"Hi," Aiden arrived and greeted her once he saw her at the café. Jolting her body, Vanessa tilted her head. *'So, it's really Aiden the Casanova?'*

"You surprised?" He asked once he saw the frown on her face. Yeah, he knew he had the nickname people keep calling him by, but the truth was... he wasn't like that. Yes, he is kind of popular among the girls, but none of them are his girlfriends. All just friends, at least that's what he says, but others who saw him will say the opposite.

"Well, yeah, a bit. However, I am not anymore," she smiles and Aiden also smiles back at her. "Shall we go now?"

"Yeah, yeah..." She hurriedly stands up and follows him to his car. The destination, they were going to is the festival that's happening in the neighbouring town. It's a funfair and near the scenic area. Both of them were enjoying their day with rides and eating all the food they sell on the stalls.

"Vanessa," He called her name while she was enjoying her dessert. "Hm?"

"Do you have any wish?"

Scrunching her eyebrows, she turned her head and saw that Aiden already lit up a small candle at the top of the muffin he bought earlier. She chuckles and her eyes turning a bit teary thinking of how sweet this guy is, but sadly this relationship will not last forever. Sniffling a bit, she hurriedly wipes the corner of the eyes. "Yeah, I do,"

"Why are you crying though?"

"Nothing, I'm just happy that you asked me my wish." She smiles and looks at him before he reaches out and softly caresses her cheek. "Make your wish now."

She closed her eyes and took a deep breath before she said inwardly, *'I wish.... You have a better life after I'm gone,'* Opening her eyes, she blows the candle and a kiss greets her lips.

"I love you," is what Aiden whispers to her before they went to check into a hotel that day.

The next day, after sending Vanessa home, he went to his friend's house and spent the weekend with his family. Vanessa didn't text him and he thought that she might be spending her day with her parents, but who knows, she went silent for a whole week.

This made Aiden a bit worried, he tried to reach her, but no reply. He finally went to her house and saw a group of people moving out the furniture from her house. He thought that Vanessa might be moving to someplace, so he tried to find her inside the house.

"Er...Excuse me,"

A middle-aged woman turning her head to the man at the door, she looks confused. "Yes?" She replied and went to him, a lot of questions started to pool in her mind at the moment she saw the man.

"Vanessa, is she here? I would like to talk to her. She hasn't contacted me for almost a week now."

The woman in front of him looked shocked when he asked her about Vanessa, "Are you Vanessa's acquaintance?"

"No, I'm her..." He stopped his word before he lowered his head a little. "her... boyfriend..," That's who he thought he was after that night.

"Oh. And she never told you anything about her illness?"

As if getting an electric shock, Aiden immediately lifted his head, "What illness?"

"Oh my God..." The woman cries and starts to tell him everything before he leaves the house soullessly. Everything feels like a dream to him, the time they had was so little that he feels God is being unfair to them.

He walked aimlessly until he finally stands in front of a gravestone. He cries silently before he kneels down and caresses the name on the gravestone. *'In loving memory, Vanessa Mendes, 1996-2019'*

14

Two Heartbroken

by Violet Evergarden

Prang!

The sound from the cashier counter made me avert my eyes to the couple who lined up in front of me. I inwardly groan a bit. I know I'm gonna be late today, and that's because of my ex. She came to my house and we had an argument before she destroyed everything in my apartment and I had to clean up the whole mess, which makes me lack sleep right now. And when I thought of having a good cup of coffee to forget everything, a couple made it to the scene, how ironic.

I watched them as the girl blushed and the guy confessed his love to her, well, I was wrong. At first I thought the two of them were like me and my ex, but they were a bloomer couple. Ha, good for them, but bad for me who is in a rush.

As they went, I immediately headed to the counter and the barista asked me if I'd registered with their new app, I said no. And she kinda urged me to download it and sign up so she could give me a free drink. I was reluctant, but I guess her smile is kind of forcing me to do whatever she wants. And, I'm in a hurry too so no time to have a debate with the young girl.

After taking my cup, I run outside and hail a taxi before one taxi stops right at the roadside. Huh! For the first time, I had luck in hailing a taxi. I smile proudly and walk to the passenger door. But as I was about to reach it, a slender hand already grabs the handle and opens it.

"Sorry," her raspy voice whispered, as she went inside the cab. I was stunned there like a statue. I blink my eyes a few times. Like, seriously? I was just......

I looked at my wristwatch before I sighed. "Guess I have to buy another drink," I went back to the café and ordered another for my boss. This could be my best excuse as to why I'm late today.

Luckily, this trick was successful. I was not yelled at and quietly made my way to my cubicle. Doing my work and starting my day. I'm working at a magazine company and I am stationed in the sales department where I need to follow up with a potential targets to expand our sales. It's no fun because at the end of the month you will be stressed out when you realize that your sales figures still haven't reached your monthly target.

Ding!

My phone got a notification; I glanced at it and noticed someone sent me a private dm. I didn't reply and another notification came in. Feeling a bit curious, I took the phone and slid it open.

I was shocked to read the text. Someone just sent me an invite for a one-night stand?? Whoa! Even though I was just breaking up with my girlfriend, it doesn't mean I want to hook up right after I get dumped, ey? So, I am replying with a "no, not interested."

I thought it would stop there, but then another series of texts came to my phone. I had to put my phone on silent and then I read the text this anonymous person has been sending me. I scrunch my eyebrow a bit. She was asking why I refused her? Why this world is unfair and why everyone treats her like she's trash. I was confused, but I couldn't ignore her messages. What if she is some psycho and decides to commit suicide? The police is surely going to ask me about it?

I think of writing something positive to her, *'As a woman, you shouldn't downgrade yourself just to be what others want you to be. You just have to be yourself and see the beauty of your life. You exist as you are, and that is enough.'*

Ding!

'You think I'm worth it? To have a beautiful life?'

I tapped my table irritated, before replying to her again.

'Everyone is entitled to the life they want. You just have to fill your life with your favorite colors. Do anything that will make you happy.'

'Will you be my friend?'

Ah this is a tough question. Where did this weird woman come from anyway? Yeah, I just realized that I didn't check where these sudden DM chats are coming from. I tapped the button to return and I sighed. It is apparently the Summer Love Café's app.

Ding! Another text comes in.

'You don't want to befriend me?'

Okay, I give up. Maybe I can give her advice and make sure she doesn't kill herself and that I will not be involved in such a case. 'No, I would love to. What's your name?'

'Belle. You can call me Belle. And you, mister?'

'Ken, just, Ken. So, um, do you frequent the coffee house?'

'I used to, but not anymore. I'm sorry about earlier. To be honest, I never asked anyone randomly like that for a one night stand. I was just.... heartbroken and desperate, maybe.'

I unconsciously chuckle a bit. And at the same time, I was relieved that she didn't intend on committing suicide as such. When she said, she's heartbroken; I suddenly remember that I'm also in the same situation as her. However, I could never think of doing something random like that.

'I see. If you feel broken and want someone to listen to your problem, you can always tell me. However, I can't promise that it will solve your problem. Maybe just lightening your burden a bit is all I can do.'

'Thanks for the comforting words. I feel a lot better now.'

And weeks passed to months and I didn't really keep track when we started talking, but the relationship I have with her started to grow, or rather, bloom? At first I thought that she might be a psycho, but no, she's a wonderful woman, she was just going through a tough phase.

We often text and call through the app, but never once did we meet up. Until one day, she sends a text to me, saying that she is moving out of town. So, before she moved she thought of meeting me for the first and last time. I guess this is it; this is where I let her go.

On the day we're supposed to meet, I make a stop at the flower stall, thinking of whether I should bring her flowers as a goodbye gift or just a give a simple hug and wave bye? I keep pondering until the florist in front of me suddenly hands me a red tulip with a smile on her face. "Better chase her while you can, young man," the florist cheered for me as I took the flower and intended to pay for the cost.

"No, it's free for you." The florist insists to not take my money. I smiled at her and thanked her before I headed to our meeting place.

The café is not too crowded and there's a free table at the corner of the shop. It is quite far from other tables which I found better as I think it has a little privacy. I went to order my drink and sat down at the table. I text Belle, saying that I'm already at the café and a minute later, she replies with an OK.

"Welcome," The worker greets someone who just entered the café and I divert my eyes to the door. A girl with glasses just came in, she had long shiny blonde hair reaching her chest and she looks really innocent. Even without layers of makeup, she looks beautiful.

I avert my eyes back and that's when my phone rings. I saw the caller ID it's from Belle and I immediately picked it up. "Hello?"

"Uh, Ken, where are you?"

"I'm at the corner table, did you arrive?" I turned my head again to the entrance door and my eyes met with the girl from before.

We both turned silent before she slowly ended the call and walked towards me. I was surprised to know that the girl who once asked me for a one-night stand is actually so innocent looking. I guess she was also shocked when she saw me because I'm not that handsome, I mean I'm just average not like some handsome CEO from a fancy novel.

"Hi," she sits down in front of me with a smile on her face. "Sorry that I ... uh, froze there for a second. The thing is, you're quite handsome," she said and tried to crack a joke.

"Oh, it's okay. I was shocked as well because you turned out to be so much more beautiful than I thought," I smile at her too. Yeah, she was much better with a smile on her face, I feel warm, warm inside my chest. Is it the feeling of comfort or just a relief that we both accept each other's appearance?

"Oh, here's a tulip for you," She gladly took it but blushed a bit. "I like the tulip. Thanks, Ken."

We talked a lot and in between she would laugh, it was a good change, to see her smiling. She's changing for the better, I guess. She's over her past bitter experience it seems. Even though it's our first-time meeting each other we both felt comfortable and there wasn't any awkwardness between us. I walked her back to her house and we stopped at the walkway to her apartment.

"So, have you packed all your things?" I started the conversation about her moving away. I know this might turn our mood a little off key, but I want to send her away with a smile.

"Yeah. I will be going tomorrow."

"Will you come back here again?"

"Hmm... I don't think so. I'm settling down there," she replied and it felt a bit hard to swallow the information I just got from her. She will be living thousands of miles away from me.

Both of us become silent for a moment before she said again, "I guess this is our goodbye then huh?" I nodded. Yeah, it seems like this is our goodbye. I hugged her and whispered in her ear, "I wish you good luck and I hope you find meaning in your life. Ah! And don't go around asking strangers the weird question you once asked me, okay?"

She chuckles and nods her head again. "Okay, but hey!" She pushes my body a little and touches my cheek, saying, "This is not the end."

"Yes, it's not," I kissed her on the lips as she savoured mine and we were like that for some time. Only stopping for us to breathe and we bid our final goodbye before I went home.

***

Six months had passed.

I was so excited once the plane landed at the airport. I couldn't wait to see her again. The love of my life, the one that I married 2 months back.

"Darling!" She ran to me once she saw me before we ended in each other's embrace.

"I'm home, babe," Yes, I changed my job and settled down with my wife at our new place, however, I would never forget the place where I first met her by accident where she steals my taxi and how we start our weird conversation on a dating app - Summer Love Café.

15

Forever In My Heart

by Amina Hazim

Online dating is not something everyone feels comfortable with, and I was one of them too. I am Jenny Cole, a twenty-six-year-old Business manager at Quinn's Enterprises, and I had been using the dating site for the past two years now. And in those two years, I have been on numerous dates, but none of them made my heart escalate, and my breathing hitch like Rodriguez Marconi, who is an Italian, and has been working in New York City for the past year as a cardiologist.

We met each other six months back, on a dating site. Forever in my heart the first time I saw him, his mesmerizing chocolate brown eyes held me captive maybe forever. But that was all the chemistry we needed, just one date for the sparks to start flying. I know I am being cliché but trust me, I have never been so much in love like this in my entire life.

"Jen? Jen? Jenny!" my best friend yelled at me from across the table, bringing me back from my thoughts into the real world, where I was having coffee with my best friend in a cute little coffee shop down-town.

"I am sorry; I think I got carried away a little." I apologized to Bella while taking a sip from my mocha.

"Yeah, right. Carried away into your dreamland where you and Mr. Prince Charming are riding on a horse." Bella replied sarcastically. I glared at her.

"I think Rodriguez will propose well before two years, Jen. Have you seen the way he looks at you?" she asks me, I give her a confused look. She huff's before continuing.

"He looks at you like you are the only woman in this entire universe, Jen. And most of the time whenever I ask him something, the question goes unanswered. And you too are in love my dear, because I have caught you smiling alone many times. So either you're in love or you're crazy!" Bella said and I just ignore her because I know what she said was true, I had fallen in love with Rodriguez a long time back.

"Fine, I do love him, but I have no idea what he feels about me." I mumbled gloomily, and Bella placed her hand over mine.

"Jen, trust me when I tell you that he will not let go of an amazing girl like you." Bella tried to console me.

"I hope so too." I replied and just then my phone chimed from an incoming message. It was from Rodriguez and unknowingly, a small smile formed on my lips.

Hi, Bellissima I will drop by at your place at seven today. Be ready. Wear something casual but elegant we are going out on a date.

The message made me instantly go on bliss.

"Look, you are doing that again." Bella said pointing at my face.

"What did I do?" I asked her.

"You are smiling for no reason. That's what I was talking about. Young love." Bella said sighing.

"So what did he say?" she asked me next.

"He wants to take me out on a date tonight." I replied and saw Bella's face turn pink with her excitement.

"Oh wow! We are going shopping. Wait! Before that how did he tell you to dress?" Bella asked.

"Uhm, casual but elegant." I replied doubtfully. I always seek help from her when I have wardrobe emergencies; after all, you should utilize the maximum benefits from your friend if she is a fashion influencer, right?

"What he meant was a frock." Bella said excitedly while dragging me towards the exit and I stagger behind her.

It took us twenty minutes to reach the mall, Bella kept blabbering about what colour would suit me, what hairstyle and so on.

"Okay first stop we will find that dream dress for your date." she said and dragged me towards a boutique that had sophisticated looking dresses on display. When we entered the shop, Bella left my hand and started rampaging through all the racks. I started browsing through a few too. One dress caught my eye it was a turquoise-coloured dress.

"Bell, how does this look?" I showed her the dress.

"I think you should have been a fashionista, you are good at this, why don't you try it on?" Bella asked me, and both of us made our way to the changing room.

"J, come on out." Bella screamed from outside. When I stepped out and when she saw me her mouth opened.

"That is the one." she said, and I agreed with her too. Once I paid for my dress, we bought shoes and came straight to my house.

"Why don't you take a shower while I arrange all your cosmetics." Bella said and I agreed.

I looked myself in the mirror and admired the perfect work that Bella did. My hair was in a half up half down bun with a few strands hanging. The dress fitted perfectly to my body and the silver heels that I bought finished the look.

"Well, looks like your carriage has arrived." Bella said when we heard the doorbell.

"Thank you so much for your help tonight Bells, I will meet up with you tomorrow." I said and she nodded before coming over and hugging me.

"Enjoy your night Jen." she said and then she went over to open the door.

"Hello, Rodriguez." Bella said hugging him.

"Have a great night and do keep Jen safe." Bella warned him and he nodded his head and took my hand leading me towards his Audi.

"You look breathtaking today, Bellissima." Rodriguez complimented.

"Thank you, so where are we heading?"

"It's a surprise." he replied and didn't give me further information even though I pestered him.

"We are here." he announced and when I looked ahead we were entering a gorgeous-looking hotel.

"Wow, Rodriguez, it's beautiful."

"Not as beautiful as you. Shall we." he said and extended his arm, and I happily obliged, grabbing his hand and, we started walking inside.

It was like I entered inside a royal fortress, the place was brightly lit with crystal chandeliers hanging, with roses everywhere and overall the place was breathtaking.

"You like it?"

"I love it." I replied with a glint in my eyes. When we were seated, the waiter brought in our menus and a bottle of white wine. So that is how we spend the rest of dinner talking about random stuff over a glass of wine. Once we were done with dinner we left the hotel.

"Do you mind taking a stroll with me under the night sky?" Rodriguez asked me. And I nodded my head. And then both of us started walking on the pavement. It was already eleven-thirty and this part of town looks deserted with a few cars passing us. After walking for twenty minutes Rodriguez stopped walking, stood near a lamp post and I looked at him in curiosity.

"Why did we stop here?" instead of giving me an answer, he got down on one knee and fished out a small jewellery box from his pocket.

"Jenny, you are the most beautiful woman I have come across in my life, and the first time I laid my eyes on you, that is when I decided that this is the woman I want to spend the rest of my life with. I love you so much Jen, would you marry me?" At that moment I was over the moon. It was as if the entire universe came to a halt.

"Yes! Yes! I will marry you Rodriguez and I love you too." I said and he gave me one of the biggest smiles, before slipping the diamond ring onto my ring finger. He got up and placed a passionate kiss on my lips.

When we broke the kiss after a minute both of us were breathing heavily. "Do you want to eat ice cream?" I nodded my head unable to speak.

"Come on," And then after looking at both sides of the road we started to cross it.

"Thank you for making me the happiest man on earth Jenny." Rodriguez said.

"Thank you to you Rodriguez, you make me so happy." I replied. If we weren't so lost in each other's eyes, we would have noticed the big SUV coming towards us.

By the time both of us looked it was too late, Rodriguez pushed me to the other side of the road, and he got hit by the car. The car kept speeding and I was screaming Rodriguez's name. People from the ice cream parlour came rushing to help us.

I stood there frozen not knowing what to do, a lady was trying to talk to me, asking me if I was ok, but I couldn't hear anything she was saying, my eyes were fixed on Rodriguez. My heart was beating at a dangerously fast pace and I kept on screaming his name, tears flowing out of my eyes. Before I knew it, I was running towards Rodriguez and knelt down beside him.

"Rodriguez, please get up. You can't leave me, I said get up." I screamed violently shaking his body. After that, everything was just a blur. The ambulance came and took Rodriguez and me to a nearby hospital. As soon as we arrived, they took him inside the operation theatre. A nurse cleaned up all my wounds and I sat in the waiting room, waiting for Rodriguez.

The operation lasted for four hours, and by that time Bella was by my side. "Jen, Rodriguez is going to be fine." she consoled me, but I was shaking, I didn't want to imagine the worse, I was trying to be positive. While I was thinking about the dinner we had earlier, I heard the door open. I abruptly got up and ran towards the doctor.

"We are sorry Miss. Jenny but the operation was not a success, he has lost a lot of blood and is currently on life support, you can talk to him, he insisted that we remove it by tomorrow. We will be transferring him to a room now so you can see him." the doctor said and then left us, it was like the worst nightmare I ever had.

"Jen, come let's go and see him." and she started leading me towards the room. When we reached the door Bella stepped aside and let me go in alone. He was hooked up to a lot of machines with bandages all over him. When I saw him like that, a lump formed in my throat, and my chest tightened.

"Jen, please don't cry. Come here." Rodriguez said in a feeble voice, and I ran over to him. He pulled me towards him and gently placed a kiss on my lips.

"Always remember I love you Jenny and don't you ever blame yourself, this was not your fault. Thank you so much for coming into my life Jen, these past six months were the best months of my life. I am happy I got to spend time with you." he said, tears streaming down his eyes while I was crying a river.

"Please move on after me Jen, but remember that I love you more than it's humanly possible." he said.

"Rodriguez, I love you too." I said in between sobs.

"I will always love you Bellissima." he whispered and I placed a kiss on his forehead.

He smiled at me before closing his eyes. I didn't want to disturb him so I left the room and Bella went in to see him. I don't know how the time flew by, but it was morning now and the doctor came back and removed his life support machine, the entire time I was holding his hand till he took his last breath.

Love was never permanent in my life, but one thing that I learned today was to cherish it while it lasted. And I did. I will always love Rodriguez till my last breath.

16

Love In The Form Of Puzzles

by Amina Hazim

Weekday mornings are always busy, with people hustling in to get something to eat before they head to work, and my bakery is no different. Clove's Bakery is situated in the heart of New York City, neatly tucked between two buildings, and it is always congested. Before the business was handed over to me, it was run by my parents. But now that I am done with my college, I took over, giving both of them a break.

"Elle, we are out of donuts." Jessica, my co-worker yelled from the kitchen.

"That is alright Jess; we are almost done for breakfast." I shouted while serving a customer his coffee. Once I was done serving the last customer his order, the place looked serene, with a few people still lingering in the shop. I relaxed a bit before heading back inside the kitchen.

"Hey, are the pastries ready for the afternoon shift?" I asked the chefs."

"Most of it is done, just a few to go." James replied, and I nodded his way before leaving the kitchen. While I was sipping my coffee, I heard the front door open, and when I looked up I saw this handsome guy wearing a suit enter the shop. He was more like a Greek God.

"Hi, can I have a cup of coffee? Take away." he asked me with his mesmerizing voice, which brought me back from my dazed state.

"Sure, Do you want anything to eat?" I asked him.

"I will have a chocolate donut." he said nonchalantly while looking around the shop.

"Five minutes Sir, I will be right back." I replied before going to prepare his order. The whole time that I was preparing his order, I felt his intense glance at me, and it made me a tad bit uncomfortable and hot at the same time.

"Here is your order," I said handing him a paper bag, and he smiled at me before taking the bag from my hand and paying for his food.

"What is your name beautiful?" he asked me. And his voice woke up unwanted feelings within me.

"Er, Elle Clove." I said stuttering. When he heard the last name, a wave of recognition crossed over his face.

"Are you the owner of this shop?" he asked with astonishment evident on his face.

"Yes and no, I am the daughter of the owners, so that technically means I am the owner after them, so yeah I am the owner." I staggered on, and he started laughing, to which I turned a shade of red due to embarrassment. Stupid Elle, why can't you even speak properly to a guy?

"You are adorable, see you around sugar pie." he said before leaving the bakery without even waiting to hear my response.

After that encounter with that handsome mystery man, whose name by the way I forgot to ask, the day in the shop was back to normal, with a few random people coming in to buy coffee. While I was browsing through my Instagram, I got a message on the dating site that I registered three weeks back. My hands started sweating when I saw the first message that I got in three weeks. I immediately opened the message to read. It was from someone named Mike Campbell.

"Hey beautiful, I would love to go out on a date with you, Saturday 6 pm at the beachfront. Would you come?"

Wow, I was over the moon now. Someone has asked me out on a date, so I instantly texted him back agreeing. And I checked his profile for his picture but to my disappointment, there was only a side profile of his face that was barely recognizable. So I texted him, "could I have a picture of yours?" I typed and pressed send. I was anxiously staring at my phone waiting for the ticks to turn blue, and it took forever for them to turn blue before he replied. My heart was in overdrive while he was typing, and when I received the message, I was disappointed.

"Let this be the old-fashioned way, I will come to see you in the next few days, and you try to guess who I am?"

He wants to play hide and seek with me, well I am up for the challenge. So I replied to him with a yes.

The next day morning, I woke up extra early and sprinted to the Bakery. By the time I arrived, Jessica was just opening the shop, and when she saw me, she looked taken aback. "Is the world spinning in the wrong orbit today?" she exclaimed.

"No. I thought of coming in early today." I replied nonchalantly and went inside the shop.

We had been serving customers for the past two hours, and I had been partly distracted to find anyone who might be Mike. But I never found anyone that might fit his description. After the morning rush I went over to a table and sat down with my coffee and phone.

"Wow, finally, the morning rush is over." Jessica beamed, coming out from the kitchen to clean the tables. I was so hurt that I could not find him today.

"Hey Elle, someone dropped a letter for you." Jessica said handing over a cream colour envelop to me. Once I took it, my heart started to escalate, could it be Mike? Without a second thought, I ripped the envelope open, and a paper fell out. I took that in my hand and turned it over to see a Picture in the front, but the picture did not make any sense. It was a picture of a hand, and the background had green grass.

While I was trying to decipher the meaning of that picture, my phone chimed in with a message, and it was from Mike.

"I think you got a part of my picture, I will drop the rest of the three pieces in the coming days respectively. Fix it, and you can know who I am."

Hmm, I didn't know he can get this creative. This game of hide and seek just got even more interesting. So that is what I waited for every day, a letter from Mike, with a missing piece from the puzzle. It was as he promised old fashioned and new.

So every day I got a part from the picture which I taped nicely. And the only part missing is his eyes but when I looked at the overall face it looked queerly familiar but I just could not figure out who.

By Friday, I was waiting for a letter but there was none and I started to get anxious. Did the letter go missing? Did someone take it? All these questions were swarming my head giving me a headache. When I was about to head back to the kitchen to get some painkillers, the front door opened and a guy came inside with a bouquet.

"Miss Clove?" he asked me.

"It is me." I replied, and then he gave me the bouquet and left the shop. The flowers were all white roses, so it took me a while to find a neatly tucked white envelope in the center of the flowers. Once I opened the letter, I took the final piece of the puzzle and fixed it with some tape, and the picture that was there gave me a shock.

This was the same guy that came into my shop a few days back, I never knew he liked me that first time we met. I was partly enraptured by his steel-grey eyes. It was the perfect shade of grey, not too light so it looks white or too dark so it looks black.

While I was admiring the picture, I saw something was written behind it, so I turned it over to read.

"Hey beautiful, I think you must have figured out by now who I am. I will be waiting for you tomorrow at the docks, don't be late." I read and a smile formed on my lips.

I don't know how the time flew by, and it is already Saturday, and I am in my room getting ready for this date. After a few final touches, I was ready, so I left my house and made my way to the docks.

I parked my car next to a shiny BMW and started walking towards the dock, the wind today was strong, and I could taste the seawater in it. The crashing of the waves with the rock gives this whole environment a serene feel.

When I was nearing the docks, I saw a silhouette of a man standing at the edge, looking at the water below. And when I moved toward him, Mike turned around with a smile on his face. "Hello, good to see you again." he said while checking me out.

"Same here." I replied with a shy smile.

"Nice outfit you got there." he said and that made my cheeks heat up with a blush.

"Thank you, you look great too." I replied.

"So, did you enjoy the past week?" he asked with curiosity laced in his voice.

"Of course, I enjoyed waiting anxiously for every letter. It was a nightmare you know." I exaggerated and he chuckled.

"I thought you were up for that kind of adventure?" he asked me.

"Yes I am up for an adventure and to be frank with you this was nice but then I think you should try something different next time because I almost got a heart attack that Friday when I did not receive a letter from you." I said with a dramatic voice.

"You are a very interesting woman." he said laughing.

"That I am." I said proudly.

"Anyway, how did you know I was on that dating site?" I asked him with one of my eyebrows raised.

"I found you two weeks back on the site, but I first wanted to know more about you and your personality before I approach you, so I started coming to your bakery regularly, and what I saw impressed me." he said.

"If you would have just texted me, then I would have told you about me, right?" I asked him.

"Well, not everyone will tell the truth." he replied with a shrug. And I agreed with him on that.

After that, both of us walked farther away from the dock while conversing with each other. Mike was an easy to go type of person and we clicked instantly. From the first time I met him, I knew I had something for him but I never knew what that was but I think time will tell what I truly feel about him. Because whenever Mike tells me something, I feel my heart flatter and I know that I might have found the right one for me.

You can rarely find true love through dating websites, but I think I may have found mine. I know it is too early to decide but when you see your other half you just know that is the person you would want to spend the rest of eternity with.

17

Modern Love

by Amina Hazim

Love can be found anywhere. Everyone has that one person in life that they call their soul mate, their other half but, whatever the name it is, in the end, love is a decision of two hearts, and that can't be achieved overnight, even through a website.

In this fast-moving life, there is very little time to fall in love in the old fashion way. So, that is why we have got dating sites now to do that job. I have always envied my parents, yearned for a love like theirs. But I don't have the time for that, so that is why I created an account on the dating website 'matchyourself.com' hoping that I will find true love just like theirs. I am Adalyn Jacob, and this is my story.

It was raining for the past couple of days, but I think today was an exception, the bright orange-yellow sun shining brightly in the clear blue sky. I have been getting ready for my date for the past two hours now, and by the time I was done; I felt the excitement and the dread slowly creep into me. This is my first date with Jack Ivashkov, whom I met on that website two months back, and ever since then, we had been texting each other, and today is the first time we are meeting.

I was starting to think maybe this is a horrible idea but, then I consoled myself by telling, it's just a meeting, no harm in that and with that I left my house on my way to the restaurant.

It took me twenty minutes, to get there and in that period I tried ditching the meeting twice but, then I made it on time.

Once I parked my car in the parking lot I made my way to the restaurant. And there in the front entrance stood a man of 6"2, sandy blonde hair wearing a grey button-up with fitted jeans. Hmm, he looks way better up close. "Hey, Adalyn?" Jack asked, sounding unsure.

"Yes, and you must be Jack?" And a small smile played on his lips.

"You are way beautiful up close." he complimented me, and my face heated up with all my blood rushed up there.

"Thank you, you don't look too bad yourself." I replied, and he smirked looking at me.

"So, shall we head inside?" he asked, and I nodded.

The inside of this place was way better than the outside. With crystal chandeliers hanging low in the ceiling and a piece of nice slow music playing in the background. Once we were seated a waiter came and took our orders and once he left we were back in silence.

The silence didn't stretch for too long before Jack spoke. "So, um, I know we haven't spoken much, but I just wanted to know whether you like me?" he asked me, and I was taken aback by his bluntness. After he didn't get any response from me, he started explaining "I know that was too quick but, err..." Jack started blabbering, it was really cute to see him all nervous, but before he could mortify himself, I interrupted him.

"No, that question was not quick, and yes, I do like you. And to be honest, I have not come across a character like you." I replied with a giggle, and I saw jack visibly relax.

"Thank you, Adalyn, I was very anxious since this is my first time doing this shit, using that app." he said nonchalantly.

"Don't worry, this is my first too. So what do you like to do in your free time?" I asked, trying to get into a comfortable conversation.

"I love going camping and traveling. What about you?"

"I love traveling as well and reading books. I always wanted to go camping but never got the chance to do that." I said with a shrug.

"Well, why don't we go camping for our next date?" Jack asked, his eyes filled with enthusiasm.

"Sure, sounds good to me." I replied. During our entire dinner, we spoke about many things, like our childhood, exes, our most embarrassing moments in life, and many more and I think in those two hours we got to know each other better. By the time we left that place, we were laughing so hard, that a random stranger would never guess that we met through a dating site.

"I enjoyed dinner with you." Jack said walking beside me.

"I never knew I would be in so much ease with a stranger." I replied and I saw Jack pouting with a sad face.

"I thought we were past that!" he replied.

"Of course, we are past being strangers. Now stop making that horrible face, it doesn't suit you." I said laughing.

"Oh, so what are we now?" Jack asked softly once my laughter died. I didn't know the answer to that either.

"What do you want us to be?"

"To be frank with you, I feel something towards you, but I don't know what that is. But I want to spend more time with you, get to know you better. And in case we don't work out we can still be friends." he replied in a serene tone. And I felt pure ecstasy and relief wash over me since I was a bit apprehensive about losing a great person like Jack.

"Thank you, Jack, and I think we will make great friends too."

"Oh, there is no doubt in that." he said with confidence. And both of us laughed and walked hand in hand towards my car.

When I went back home I took a shower before laying on my bed thinking about all the events that happened today. Jack was a great guy, I liked the way he listens to whatever I say before replying, as far as I have seen, most of the guys I know don't have the patience to sit and listen and have a normal conversation or even try to get to know each other. I know I have started liking Jack, but it is too early for me to decide about my feelings.

The next day I was getting ready to head to work, while I was applying my makeup, my phone chimed with an incoming message, so once I was done applying my lipstick, I took my phone to check the message. It was from Jack.

"Hey, are you still up for that camping date?"

"Sure, I would love to; send me the date and place and I will be there." I replied.

"We will go this Saturday, and I will come to pick you up at nine in the morning." he replied

"Sure sounds great to me." I replied before keeping my phone inside my purse and heading outside my house.

After a long day at work, I came back home exhausted to see a bouquet of pink and white flowers at my doorstep. I picked them up and took a sniff. hmm, the smell of fresh flowers always calms me down. I took the flowers inside and removed the ribbon wrapped around it to place them inside a vase, and when I did that, a note dropped on the floor. That is strange I thought there was no sender. I placed the flowers in the vase filled with water and took the paper to read it.

"Hi, Adalyn hope you like the bouquet. Those are from my garden, they were there too long without someone to take care of them. Hope you take good care of them. ;)"

Jack...

The flowers were from Jack. I didn't expect that. This guy is giving me a new reason every day to like him even more.

It was already Friday night and I was busy packing for the camping trip that we are going to tomorrow; I was bewitched and jittery in equal parts. This is the first time I am going camping and that too with a boy all alone in the middle of nowhere, it does sound thrilling but scary at the same time too.

"Are you ready for tomorrow?" I received a message from Jack.

"As ready as I can be. I will meet you tomorrow, good night." I replied back and after a few seconds, I got a reply.

"Great, sleep tight." and that is exactly what I did. Thinking about tomorrow took me into a dream filled with adventure and a bit of romance at the end.

I woke up the next day to the sound of my alarm blaring next to my ears. I took a shower and I made myself a sandwich and sat on the kitchen island to eat my breakfast. Once I cleaned the kitchen, I took my phone and backpack and went into my living room to wait for Jack.

After fifteen minutes of waiting, I heard the doorbell ring, so I got up from the couch and went to answer the door. "Hi, are you ready?" Jack was wearing a black tee-shirt with cargo shorts.

"Yes, I am ready I just have to lock the place." I replied and I went inside my house and took my backpack. After locking the house, we got into Jack's car and drove off.

We spend two hours driving before we reached the wilderness. There was a sign attached to a tree that said camping site and there were a few cars parked there with people swarming around them. After taking out our backpacks from the trunk, Jack locked the car and started walking towards the forest.

"I know a great place where we can set up a camp, but we might have to walk for about forty minutes to reach that place. Or there is another camping site which is just a twenty minutes walk. Where would you like to go?" Jack asked while stepping over broken branches.

"If the scenery is exceptional then I don't mind walking for forty-five minutes." I replied and Jack smirked at me, liking my decision, so that is where we went. The forest was damp with mud puddles here and there. The birds atop trees chirping blissfully gave the forest a sense of tranquillity. Neither of us spoke, instead, we were both enjoying the intrinsic beauty of the forest. I didn't know how time flew by. Till I heard Jack say "we are here." the place was magnificent, there was a waterfall that was near the camping site with the sun shining brightly on top, making the water glimmer. Once I was done admiring the place, I helped Jack set up our tent.

"All done, I will start up the fire now, and then we are good for the night." Jack said, and then he went over to collect some dried woods, while I arranged our sleeping bags inside the tent. When everything was set and when the night came by, both Jack and I snuggled up near the campfire roasting marshmallows. The wind started to get cold by the minute so I moved closer to Jack and that small gesture made him look at me. His eyes held so many different emotions, and the one prominent emotion was love.

"Adalyn, these past few days talking to you, I realized that I like you more than a friend, and I would love it if you would be my girlfriend?" Jack asked with uncertainty.

"I do like you more than a friend too, Jack." I replied sincerely, and his eyes sparkled at my word. And without a second thought, I kissed him.

Love is not only an emotion but it's also a catalyst that forms a new relationship. Be it love, friendship, etc... Whatever it is, if there is no love in it, then there is no relationship either. No matter what technology brings in the future to find love, you will only fall in love with that one person you are destined to. And no amount of modern technology can change that.

18

Unexpected Love

by C.L. Williams

After months of failed dates and the nagging of his friends, Victor agrees to set up a profile on an online dating site. After searching through every site, app, and pages on social media, Victor settles on trying the dating site/app called *Let's Try Love*. It has the highest review scores of any site he checked and it's both a website and an app, that way, he can check the app when he is on his lunch break and look at the website when he is at home. He also plans to look at it on his computer at work, whenever his boss isn't around. He sets up everything and within minutes, Victor already has five messages in his inbox. Victor isn't a pessimistic person, but he knows he's not the best-looking guy on the planet. For four women to message him immediately after setting up his account, he's a little surprised.

The first message read *Hey baby! Wanna have some fun?* Victor is unimpressed and deletes the message. The second message was from a woman named Diana, it was a simple hand-waving emoji. Victor decides to check out her profile after he reads the remaining two messages.

The third message is from a girl named Yuri. He looks at her picture and he thinks Yuri is cute. Her message reads *We should talk sometime*. Victor decides to respond to Yuri before moving on to the next message. He responds with *You're very cute in your picture, I'm down to talk*. He then moves on to the final message, a girl named Victoria. Victor thought it was funny his name being Victor and hers being Victoria. Her message simply read, *Hey sexy* . He replies with *Hello sexy yourself :D!* After answering the last two messages, he's about to respond to Diana, the girl that simply sent a hand-waving emoji. Before he can respond, he gets a response from Yuri. Her response to him calling her cute; *LOL Thanks sweetie! It's my senior pic! Took them last month* . Victor sees her saying it's her senior picture and decides he is not responding to her. He goes back to Diana's message and says, *Hello Beautiful! We should talk sometime.* Victor isn't expecting much of a response. He knows he lacks flirting skills and his previous messages were a possible underage girl, a guy pretending to be a girl, and someone he's sure is only interested in a hook-up. Much to Victor's surprise, Diana responds him.

She responds; *WOW! You're the first guy to respond to me that is not asking for sex!* Victor laughs to himself knowing he was thinking Diana was about to ask for sex as well. He responds to Diana, *I'm looking for a real relationship, not some random hook-up with some girl I don't know.* He then sends the message and before Victor can continue looking at other profiles, he gets another message from Diana, *Where do you live? Last guy I tried talking to lives 50 miles away from me.* Victor reads the message and responds *Trekton and I work in Enterprise.* Seeing that Diana is responding quickly to him, Victor quits looking at other profiles and waits for Diana to respond. He is not let down, *OMG! I live and work in Enterprise!* Victor is finally to a point where he feels bold enough to ask *Since I work in Enterprise and you live in Enterprise, would you like to do dinner this week? I like eating at this place called Outpost.* Victor sends the message and sees that he has a message from Victoria, the only other girl to send him a message that he didn't find weird or creepy, but he also wanted to see if Diana will respond.

Even though it was only a few minutes, Victor felt like he had been waiting hours when he got a response from Diana, *I LOVE OUTPOST* followed by multiple smiling heart emojis. She then sends another message *Is Friday good for you?* Victor smiles as he knows he is about to have his first date in almost two years, he responds with *Friday sounds good. Is seven good for you?* He sends it and sits there again anxiously waiting for a response from Diana. Again, even though Victor is only waiting a few minutes, his anxiety makes it feel that he is waiting for hours. She then responds with *7 sounds good! See you there. I'll be wearing a red dress, that way you know who to look for.* Victor did not realize it until she said what she plans to wear but Diana is not using her own picture for her profile picture. She's using an animated character for her profile picture. Victor then makes a run to his closet, looks inside, and runs back to his laptop to give his response. *I bet you look good in that red dress, I'll be wearing a black polo. See you Friday!* He sent the message and smiles to himself. He can say he finally has a date and with someone who lives nearby. Even though Victor has his concerns about Diana not using her own picture for her profile, he is not going to complain given he has had very little luck leading up to Diana responding to him.

***

Friday is here and Victor is putting on his black polo and is getting ready to make the travel from Trekton to Enterprise for his date with Diana at Outpost. Victor goes to the hostess and requests his table, he informs her his date will be here momentarily. As the hostess is leading Victor to his table for his date with Diana, he notices something. He is one of many guys in the restaurant wearing a black polo. Victor feels he needs to inform

Diana about the issue, but he is currently without her number. He's been using the Let's Try Love website, not the app. Victor quickly opens up the app store on his phone and rapidly goes through each app until he finds Let's Try Love. He finds it and begins downloading the app. While waiting for the app to download, he looks around to see if Diana has arrived yet. He does not see anyone wearing a red dress and resumes staring at his phone in hopes of the app downloading faster. The app is done downloading and Victor types in his log in information. He notices he has one unread message from Diana, Sorry sweetie, I'm running late. Victor responds, It's all good. BTW, I'm one of many dudes here wearing a black polo. I'll be looking for you. I'll stand up when I see you. I'm about 6'2, kinda skinny, and I wear glasses. I've already got us a table. Victor hits send and impatiently awaits a response from Diana.

Victor places his phone on the table as a waitress comes over to ask for his order. He tells her he would like a glass of water until his date arrives. After the waitress leaves to get Victor his water, his phone's notification tone begins buzzing. He picks it up and it's Diana. She responds with, I'll message you when I'm at the door. That way you'll know when to stand up. OMW! Victor responds with a thumbs up emoji and the waitress returns with his glass of water. When she hands him the glass of water, Victor asks if she can bring two menus to the table before his date gets here. She smiles and walks away to grab the menus.

Victor is waiting for the waitress to return with the menus when his phone goes off. He checks and it's Diana *I'm here! You can stand up now. LOL.* Victor stands up and even though Diana didn't put a picture of herself on her profile, Victor can already tell Diana is easily the most beautiful woman he's ever been on a date with. He stands up and notices his nerves are getting the better of him and he feels he is starting to sweat. Diana sees Victor in his black polo, noticeably tall stature, and glasses. She smiles at him as she walks over to him. She automatically goes in for a hug and begins talking.

"Hello, I'm Diana." She says, starting off the conversation, followed by a smile that can make any man melt.

"Hi. Victor," Victor says in a speedy tone as they end the hug and sit down. "I've got to be honest, I'm feeling a bit nervous."

"Why?" She asks.

"I was not expecting the most beautiful woman in the room to be my date for the evening. You look amazing." Victor says as he gives a crooked smile to Diana.

"Thanks." She responds as she blushes from the compliment courtesy of Victor.

Victor is about to say something, but the waitress comes over and hands menus to Victor and Diana. Seeing the woman Victor is with, the waitress whispers in his ear, "She's pretty"

The two look at their menus for a moment before Victor breaks the ice with an unusual conversation starter. "If you don't mind me asking, why is someone as beautiful as you using a dating site? I could see men throwing themselves at you."

"Well, I have a job that requires a lot of my time and so many men talk a big game but when the time comes to step up, they just can't. Why did you resort to online dating, and what made you pick *Let's Try Love*?" Diana asks.

"I've been single for a while and my friends are giving me a hard time about it. Like you, I work a lot. I don't consider myself good-looking, so I thought I'd go for the anonymity of online dating. I chose *Let's Try Love* because it had the best review scores of the other sites, and it had the highest scores of any site/app hybrid." Victor responds.

"I think you're cute, and you've been more of a gentleman than any other date I've had recently. Where do you work if you don't mind me asking?" Diana asks.

"Data analytics at Troi office park."

Before Victor can say anything else, Diana interrupts him. "Did you just say you work in the Troi office park?"

"Yeah, why?"

"I work in Office Q over there! How have I never seen you before?" Diana asks in excitement.

"I go in, do my job, and leave. None of my friends work there and other than my boss, I can't say I'm close with anyone there."

"Well, come Monday, you and I will be having lunch. What time do you usually take lunch? That way I can coordinate my schedule."

"I usually go around one, that way I can go somewhere *after* the craziness of a lunch rush."

"Tell me about it," Diana says, "I went to lunch around noon ONCE, a mistake I'll NEVER make again." She then concludes her venting with some laughter.

Diana and Victor share a laugh before the waitress comes back over to take their orders. Diana orders some pasta and a sparkling water while Victor orders a burger and a soda. After the waitress leaves, Diana asks Victor something about what she noticed.

"Usually I see guys order a beer with their food." Diana says to Victor.

"I live in Trekton and I didn't know if you drove or not. I don't want to take any chances. Can I ask you the same thing?" Victor asks.

"This may surprise you, but...." Diana pauses, "I don't drink."

"Not too surprising, I know plenty of people that don't drink."

The waitress comes back with their orders and their drinks. Diana and Victor spend the rest of the evening engaged in small talk and enjoying the food they are eating. At the end of the date, Diana gives Victor her number. That way the two of them can talk without needing to go onto *Let's Try Love*. She tells Victor to text her when he arrives home. Victor pays for the meal and he walks Diana to her car. They talk for a brief moment before Diana kisses Victor and gets in her car to go home. Victor then heads to his car and makes his way back home. As promised, he texts Diana when he gets home, letting her know he has arrived home safe. The two text one another for the majority of the night.

Monday is now here, and Victor is at work; Data Analytics at Troi Office Park. While he is finishing up some work on his computer before going to lunch, his boss stops by his cubicle.

"Hey Victor, there's someone here for you. She said you promised her lunch." Victor's boss says in a confused tone.

"Thanks Bruce," Victor says to his boss, "I'm almost done, then I'm going to lunch."

"Victor," Bruce says in a serious tone, "Ever since I became president of Data Analytics, I've never known anyone to come here to see you, especially someone that gorgeous. Just save what you're doing, take some extra time for lunch. Don't worry about pay." Bruce then steps aside and makes a phone call. Within a few minutes, he returns and pulls out his wallet. He gives Bruce fifty dollars in cash, "Victor, there's this nice steak diner on Riker Street. I already have your reservation set up. Here's some cash. Now take your time on the date and make that woman happy."

"You don't have to do this Bruce." Victor says, feeling uncomfortable about taking the money and the reservation from his boss. "I'm just taking her somewhere for lunch. We can do something when we're not on a time clock."

Bruce, insistent that Victor take the deal, replies, "I told you, don't worry about pay and I think this will help. Trust me!" Bruce says as he holds out the money once more.

Victor accepts the offer from Bruce. He saves everything he needs on his necessary reports. He then goes outside of the Data Analytics office and Diana is standing outside the office door, waiting on him.

"Sorry it took so long, my boss took one look of you and said I needed better lunch plans. Gave us a reservation for some steak diner on Riker Street." Victor tells Diana.

"You mean your boss wants you to take me to House of Glory Steakhouse?!" Diana says in shock.

"I guess so, I'm not in that part of the city too much. I know how to get there, but I've never been much of a steakhouse person."

"Don't worry about that, they have other amazing food. You do know we'll be more than an hour in there?"

"My boss told me I *need* to leave a good impression with you and to take as much time as I need. He even told me that I'll still get paid." Victor tells Diana.

"All I need to hear, let's go!" Diana responds as they walk over to the parking garage and get in Victor's car.

They go to the House of Glory Steakhouse and end up spending three hours at the steakhouse. When they get back, Bruce, Victor's boss is at the main entrance of Troi Office Park waiting to see how things went for his employee.

"So......," Bruce says with a cheesy grin upon his face.

Diana responds before Victor can say anything, "It was great, and my boyfriend told me I have you to thank!" Diana says as she extends her hand to Bruce.

Bruce is complimenting Diana while Victor stands in shock that not only is his boss happy for him about his date, Diana just referred to him as her boyfriend. While in a state of shock, Bruce then snaps Victor out of his trance.

"VICTOR!" Bruce yells.

"Sorry boss, what's up?" Victor asks.

"Take the rest of the day off. Take Diana to your place and enjoy the evening. If you need tomorrow off," Bruce then gives Victor a wink, "That's fine by me!"

"Thanks boss!" Victor and Diana make their way back to the parking garage, before Victor can give Diana directions to his house, Diana gives him directions to hers. He then follows her to her place and the two of them sit in the living room and watch movies while engaging in some small talk.

"Diana, things have been going very well for us. Is something bad about to happen?" Victor asks.

"No! I think we both found what we're looking for. You need someone who understands you have a busy lifestyle with work, and I need someone who is interested in me and not just getting me into bed, by the way, you won't have to wait too much longer on that," Diana says as she smiles at Victor and follows it up with a kiss.

"Sooooo," Victor says as he tries to tell Diana what is on his mind, "I guess me asking what I need to ask is not going to be a problem then."

"What would that be?" She asks.

"With everything going well and you calling me your boyfriend to my boss, I think I should go ahead and delete my profile on *Let's Try Love.*"

"Good idea!" Diana then gets up and races to her bedroom. She then comes back into the living room with her laptop, opens it up, and makes her way to the website. She then logs into the site, goes to account settings, and requests delete profile. When she was prompted to explain why, she replies with OTHER, in the comments section, Diana responds, "Met the man of my life in Victor. He's charming, sweet, and everything I could ever ask for. I'm deleting my profile because Let's Try Love truly worked!" She then hits send and her account is now deactivated. Diana then hands her laptop to Victor who also chooses to delete his profile. When asked why, Victor responds, "I tried the website because my friends kept harassing me to. What I never expected was that I would meet Diana, she's beautiful on the outside and her inner beauty surpasses that. Let's Try Love is a true success and I will be happy to recommend it to all of my single friends." Victor then hits send and his profile is now deactivated. He then gives Diana the laptop and she puts it away and the two of them resume watching their movie.

Shortly after both of them deleted their accounts, Victor's phone starts buzzing. He checks his phone to see he has an unread email. He reads it to himself before reading it to Diana. The email reads:

Hello Victor,

This is Adam, co-founder of Let's Try Love. I just read your reason for deleting your profile and while it's upsetting to lose someone, my wife and I could not help but notice how quickly you and Diana met one another using our website. With her permission, I'd like to ask if you and her can submit a picture of the two of you for us to put on our website as a way to show those in doubt that Let's Try Love can work?

Thank you,

Adam

Victor then asks Diana, "Wanna take a pic of us for them to put on the site?"

"YES!" Diana says before pulling out her phone for a quick picture of her and Victor. She snaps two quick pictures; one of them smiling and one of them kissing. She then texts the pictures to Victor, who in return replies to Adam of *Let's Try Love*. Victor puts his phone down and resumes his cuddling and movie watching with Diana before his phone starts buzzing once more. It's another email from Adam of *Let's Try Love*.

Victor, it's Adam again. My wife loves the picture you sent me. I'll be doing a site update later this week. When the picture of you and Diana is added to the homepage, I'll contact you again, that way the two of you can see it and give your approval.

Thanks again,

Adam

"This is exciting," Diana says, "I've never been featured on a website before," She then moves in to kiss Victor, "And I get to be featured on this website with you." Diana then looks Victor deep into his eyes and says, "Victor, I love you."

"I love you too, Diana," He then moves in to kiss Diana once more. The two continue watching the movie on television before both of them eventually fall asleep on the couch with Diana wrapped in Victor's arms.

EPILOGUE

Victor and Diana eventually see their picture on the *Let's Try Love* homepage. It remains part of the homepage for nearly a year. Around the time their picture goes down to show off the new couples that have found love. Victor decides the time is right and proposes to Diana. While the two of them never thought online dating was the best option, they found love with one another and have *Let's Try Love* to thank for the reason that they found love.

19

One Day, Two Dates

by Ishika Jain

Austin didn't like it. He didn't like it at all.

And he made sure that Scarlett was aware of it.

"Austin." She sighed as she put on some concealer. "Why are you making such a big deal out of this?"

"Because it is dangerous. Unsafe. Stupid. And did I mention... dangerous?" He exasperated. He was a firm believer of the fact that if he continued repeating the same thing every minute, it would somehow drill itself into Scarlett's brain, and ultimately the 'dread date' will be prevented.

"Yes. About a million times now." She deadpanned as she turned and gave him a look.

"Doesn't mean it isn't true!" He was losing it, and he knew it.

He mentally cursed that online dating app, whichever one Scarlett had been using for the past one month. That stupid, idiotic app that had made Scarlett a phone addict and had collided her path with some.... moron online.

He was trying to sweep the fact that he had feelings for her under the rug, by acting like an overprotective best friend. He had hoped through that pretension, he could even manage to convince himself that 'it' was nothing, but it was clear as day he was doing a piss poor job of it.

Scarlett's gaze softened as she looked at her best friend. She closed the steps separating them both and sat on her bed beside Austin.

"Look, I know you are worried. And I would be too if the roles were reversed." She started as she took his hand in hers. Austin's heart involuntarily picked up its pace. "But trust me when I tell you that this guy, he is just amazing. He is everything I want in a boyfriend."

She had a dream-like look on her face as she told him this and he covered his pained expression with a well-rehearsed smile.

"I get it Scar." He murmured and she looked him in the eye. "Just... I don't know. I guess it's fine." He relented.

And how could he not? Looking at her, as her eyes shined bright with hope, he just had to give in to her wishes.

God, she had no idea of the effect that she had on him.

Scarlett beamed and threw her arms around him. Holding him tight as she lightly swayed them.

Austin's arms hung limp on his sides. He knew, if he wrapped them around her, there was no way he would have let her go anytime soon.

"Thank you." She mumbled against the crook of his neck and pulled back.

Austin gulped and forced another smile her way.

She hopped up and went back in front of the mirror.

Deciding he might as well kill the silence and the pain in his chest, he asked her just as she started dabbing blush on her cheeks.

She had never worn this much amount of makeup before and even though it was making her look beautiful, he preferred her without it.

"Where are you guys going anyway?"

As if he had told her about a Macy's sale (which she loved), she brightened up.

"Oh, he is taking me to Stellar's." She gushed and he raised his eyebrows.

"That posh restaurant on the outskirts of town?" He confirmed and she nodded.

"But- I thought you guys were-" He stammered in utter confusion and she interrupted him.

"Yes, I know. I wanted that too but Stellar's isn't bad, is it?" She asked him with a smile and he didn't bother to give her a reply.

Scarlett had stumbled upon a guy named Luca, a Latino on that online dating app.

In the beginning, she had joked off with Austin saying how fun it was to flirt with people online and then break their hearts. Austin used to have a good laugh at that and sometimes he would even sit with her while she flirted with different guys at the same time just for fun.

But it all had changed two weeks earlier when she had started talking to a guy named Luca online, who had a shirtless mirror selfie as his profile pic and the mobile covered his face so it wasn't visible and contrary to Scarlett's beliefs Austin was convinced he was an ugly piece of shit.

Of course, it was his personal reason to think and wish and assume that, but hey- no one could be sure!

Anyways, Luca had managed to charm Scarlett in his own way. She had of course flirted with him as she did with other guys, but unlike the other responses, Luca had been so humble throughout the chat.

It had intrigued Scarlett, who was a sheer flirt by heart and Luca was probably the first one who hadn't fallen into the trap of her suggestive words.

Another thing about Scarlett was, that she was a nerd. And never had a boyfriend till date, even though she was 17 already. So seeing her like this was totally new for Austin.

Austin however wasn't a nerd, but he never had a girlfriend either. Mainly because he was in love with Scarlett.

Just two weeks of texts, and here Scarlett was getting ready for her first date with a guy she didn't even know.

Well at least according to Austin because Scarlett was convinced both of them were made for each other and knew everything about each other.

That fact didn't sit well with Austin because if they did know each other that well, then Luca should know that ever since Scarlett was 12 she had dreamed of going to a drive-in theatre for her first date and watching One Day, her favorite movie.

He didn't trust Luca. Even though Scarlett had basically declared that it was safe, Austin wasn't going to be naive.

He knew what could happen. She had never met the guy. He could be a rapist for all they knew.

And even if he wasn't, where was the guarantee that Luca wouldn't manipulate his innocent Scar into sleeping with him? What if he forced his lips on her and stole her first kiss tonight?

Austin's blood boiled at the thought. He would kill that son of a bitch if he did something bad to Scarlett.

But as fate had decided, he didn't have to do anything of that sort. Not tonight.

Because as it turns out, Scarlett had called Austin halfway through her date.

She had been hiding in the bathroom, trying to keep her tears at bay as she phoned her best friend and asked him to get her.

"He was shamelessly flirting with our waitress." She hiccupped as she got in Austin's car after sneaking through the back. She didn't even feel an ounce of regret for leaving Luca like that. "He thinks he has the money and the looks that he can do whatever he wants. Taking one girl on a date and eyeing another one in front of her." She ranted. "And he is such a douchebag. He is totally different in real life. For one, he isn't humble like at all."

"He didn't even remember I don't eat pork and instead ordered that for me. You were right Austin. People aren't who they seem. Especially when you meet them online."

Austin sighed and let her talk her feelings out.

Though he hated Luca, he was selfishly also glad about what he had done.

Because what he did, gave Austin the perfect opportunity to finally face his feelings.

Stopping his car at the last row of cars in the Drive-In Theatre, he turned to Scarlett who was already looking around confused.

"Scar." He started and turned a bit to properly look at her. She had been dressed to perfection today and he couldn't deny that. "You look beautiful tonight. And it would be a shame if this dress up of yours would go to waste because of that Latino bastard."

Scarlett's breath hitched as she noticed where he was going with his words.

She didn't know why her heart started thumping at an incredible speed at that realisation, but she didn't hate it at all. If anything, she was anticipating his next words with everything in her and that scared and bedazzled her at the same time. Who knew that her crush on her best friend-the cute dork- had never really faded away?

"So, Scarlett Marie Brown, will you give me the pleasure of taking you on your first dream date?"

She didn't know why a lone tear escaped her eye, but it did and she hastily wiped it before giving Austin a watery smile.

"Why yes, of course. But this wouldn't be my dream date." She said as she put her hand in Austin's, her heart beating incredibly fast.

"Why?" Austin furrowed his eyebrows.

"Because they aren't playing One Day tonight." She said and Austin laughed out loud.

The sound was melodious to her ears.

Giving her a teasing wink, he answered back. "Oops. Then maybe we'll have to do this again on the day they do play One Day."

20

Never-Ending Sunday

by Nafisa Faruque

It was a sunny Sunday when I first saw him in the park a few minutes away from my home, sketching under a tree. Taking quick steps, I rushed to his side.

"Excuse me?"

He looked at me with annoyance plastered on his face; and that was when I realized that I had mistaken him as my date.

I was about to apologize, but then I looked into his eyes.

I looked into those big, blue; teary eyes of his and I just kept looking. That was until he decided to break the eye contact to blink away his tears. He gave me one last look, before standing up and walking away.

I was watching him leave until my phone made a sound. The screen showed a notification from the dating app I had started using a few weeks prior to that day.

"Sorry, I can't make it."

I remember rolling my eyes to that.

I spent that Sunday morning writing in my diary about this weirdly intriguing guy I met under the tree. For some unknown reasons, thoughts of him kept dancing on my mind that whole week.

I wanted to see him again.

As another Sunday arrived, he being there under the same tree had made the afternoon eventful. I recall finding it difficult to walk any further, and I knew I had to talk to him.

I forced my legs to move. There, I stood in front of him, knowing I had to say something; anything.

He was looking up at me with his thick brows furrowed. Gulping hard, I blurted out a simple "Hi" and in response, I received a blank look from him.

Nodding, I had taken it as a sign to leave. But as I turned, he had called out to me: "Wait!" He low-key yelled out.

Being someone who gets scared easily, I flinched at his call. He was already staring at me when I looked back.

"What's your name?" He asked after a long pause, displaying a hint of hesitation.

That was the start of a conversation that lasted till late evening; from asking other's names to cracking jokes together. We had forgotten how we were strangers just that morning.

I had come back home with a smile that evening; a smile that reminded me that although his was so alluring, yet it was lacking something.

We would meet up every Sunday under that same tree and talk through the weeks over texts and calls. A month had passed and I was still unable to find in his smile that mystical feeling that I had seen in his eyes the first time we met. Whenever he'd smile at me, I'd feel a pang in my chest because his smiles always seemed incomplete; it was like he was holding something back, burying it deep within and not allowing it to show.

Out of curiosity, I asked him one Sunday why he was crying on our first meeting.

His grip on my hand suddenly loosened as he sat up straight, touring his eyes away from the stars that were glowing in the sky. I followed his actions before staring at his side profile. I had a frown on my face because he would only gaze at me from the corner of his eyes.

I tried to put my right hand on the back of his left one, when he proceeded to amuse me further by yanking my approaching hand away.

He mumbled a quiet "I have to go" prior to running out of the park without throwing even a quick glance at my frozen state.

It felt like time stopped when he disappeared from my sight.

After having a small debate in my mind, I came to the conclusion of not running after him and that is something I regret the most.

Weeks after weeks passed after that, and I spent the first few Sundays waiting for him under that tree.

That tree, I had never really paid much attention to it as I had in those Sundays. It was tall in height, tall enough to protect me from the burning rays of the sun. The rustling of its leaves were like tunes of comfort. Whenever I'd cry sitting under the tree, it'd let a few of its greenish leaves brush delicately over my head before they fell to my lap. On some Sundays, I'd fall asleep with my back against its thick stem and it would stay so calm; allowing me to have my much needed rest.

The longer the wait turned out to be, the fewer days became that I'd spend waiting for him. Yet one question was still lingering in the back of my mind: Why did he do that?

I continued with my usual life. The only thing lacking was him, but I had grown over the emptiness; or so I thought.

It was another Sunday evening. I was on my bed with my earphones in, wondering if I should order in or not when I received a text from him and my heart almost leaped out of my chest. I was confused and even though I refused to accept it at that moment, but deep down I felt so happy seeing his message.

It was when I anxiously clicked on the notification that my heart stopped beating for a minute or so.

"I'm dying!!"

I read out the text message a few times to believe what I was seeing, below was given the address of a hospital.

I recollect how I did not think about anything at all before grabbing my coat, sprinting down the stairs and out of the house; slamming the door shut behind me.

It had started raining while I was in the cab. The shut windows had only allowed the faint sound of rain in along with the soft obnoxious whispers that I had tried my best to ignore all the way from home to the hospital.

But when my eyes for the very first time in months fell over his form laid on a stretcher being dragged towards the operation theatre; I broke down. I wasn't able to hold myself together; I had to let it out. I had been strong for too long.

Even today, I continue to stand tall just how he would have wanted me to; as I find myself once again in the all too familiar graveyard, staring right at his name engraved into the gravestone.

Destiny played its game to bring us together, while fate played one of its own to cut off the strings; yet one still remains. Although his connection to this world has come to its end, yet his connection to me will remain strong as long as there exists a Sunday.

You will forever be my never-ending Sunday.

21

Coincidental Dating

by Ishika Jain

"Okay, so you are cancelling on me. That's great! Now I have no one to go with to the Urdu Poetry Festival tomorrow!"

I hung up my phone angrily on my friend, Ankur, who cancelled the plan just a night prior to the festival because of some work.

Ankur called back dreading my temper and as soon as I picked up the call, he started apologising, "I am so sorry Janvi. I got a very urgent work at this last moment, I too wanted to come."

"Ankur, this is not done, now I have no one to go with. What will I do there alone? I really wanted to listen to Nizami Brother's Qawaali but now I will have to cancel." I croaked.

"Please, don't cancel your plan because of me, go there, enjoy and anyway you love poetry so much that you won't need anyone else for enjoyment." Ankur was continuously trying to cheer me up.

I desperately wanted to go there and had been waiting for this poetry festival for so long. So, I finally agreed that I would not cancel my plan and would go and enjoy by myself. It's not like I don't go out alone. In fact, I have been to many events by myself and I was happy to go alone to that event also but, it's just that I was mad at Ankur for cancelling the plan at the last moment as he did this once before also. But, at last I was happy that I would listen to Nizami Brothers and their melodious Qawaali, specially, "KunFayaKun".

Usually, I spend my free time in reading novels and poetry books or myself writing some poems or sometimes I watch movies but that day, my mind was not settling at any chore. I was lying idle on my sofa cum couch and it was around 11 o' clock at night. Being a night owl, the night had just begun for me. So, sleeping was not even an option.

I have a strange habit that whenever I am feeling extremely bored, I scroll through my play store in phone and look for different apps, download them to see their application and then uninstall them or sometimes keep them if I find them useful. I know, it's a weird habit but it's interesting. I get to see what's out there in digital market.

So, as I was scrolling, I saw an intriguing app, far different from my "suggestions for you" list, it was a dating app! I read about it, read the reviews and got excited, what if I download it once just to check how these dating apps work as people have hyped these apps so much but I never had an experience with such apps. So, to try out new things in the wave of my early 20s, I downloaded it and made my profile.

Soon my phone was flooded with notifications that some xyz liked your profile, some xyz wants to send you message. It was really shocking for me that how quick it was. I accepted one or two requests after checking their profile and we got into talking. For the first time in my life, I was using the dating app!

It was hard to believe, even for me. I recalled how I used to mock these apps. I selected the app and was dragging it to delete option but then something stopped me in between. I wanted to experience it more.

Those one two chats were casual like what do you do and all but then I thought that maybe, I too should check out the news feed, i.e., the boys and see how it works from this side. So, as I was scrolling, I saw many boys but didn't send them request or liked their profile but then I thought, Janvi, why are you being such a loser, you can send a request, it's not a big deal!

And the moment I thought that yes, I would send request to someone, I had Sagar's profile on my screen. I read his profile and it seemed pretty decent so I liked his photo and then got indulged in viewing profile of those guys who liked my profile.

Few minutes later, I got a text from Sagar, "Hey, you there?"

"Hi, how are you?" I replied.

And hence, our conversation started.

Pretty soon, we got to know about each other and it was surprising to know that we both have done Mathematics Hons. from Delhi University. We both were in North Campus, i.e., our colleges were just a kilometre away from each other and it was so shocking to know that we were in same batch, 2015-18. As we continued talking, I found out that we had so much in common. His face looked very familiar and then few minutes later, we realised that we had already met. Or not met but had seen each other around the campus. We used to go to each other's college a lot for fests and competitions, that too during same years.

I mean, was this destiny or something, I don't know! Who thought that years after, we would interact this way on a dating app!? I got totally engrossed in talking to him and forgot about checking out other profiles and chats.

I asked him, "For how long have you been using this dating app?"

"Since the last half an hour", he replied.

My eyes got widen seeing such a coincidence because that's when I installed this app. I got more curious and elated.

"Have you used such apps before or been on date through these?" I asked anticipating his response.

"No", his reply was flashing on my screen. I couldn't believe the odds. It was a new experience for both of us and I grew comfortable in talking to him because of all such similarities. He truly seemed like a genuine amiable guy. Oh, it was so awesome! I loved the coincidences.

Soon after, he asked, "Do you want to meet someday?"

I replied in teasing tone, "Are you asking me out for a date?"

"Maybe yeah"

"Then ask properly like a guy asks a girl". I chuckled and my face turned pink. In few hours, we had reached that stage where I could totally pull his leg.

"Okay, so Janvi, would you like to go out on a date with me?"

"Sagar, I would love to go out on a date with you! But when?" My heart was somersaulting with excitement.

"I am free tomorrow and day after, now you tell, when do you want to?"

On hearing him being free tomorrow, that Urdu poetry festival popped up in my mind because of which I was yelling at Ankur few hours back and didn't want to go alone.

So, I asked him, "Do you have interest in poetry?"

"Not much, just a bit", he replied.

And regardless of his answer, I put my proposal foreword, if he would like to go to Urdu poetry festival with me. I thought that he would say no but to my surprise he accepted.

We got into talking few hours back for the first time and now we had a date just the next day. It was like running a marathon for a slow runner like me who once spent years in confessing feelings to her school-time crush. We talked till 3 am that night and next day I had a date, my first date from such dating apps with the only guy whom profile I liked. I couldn't sleep with excitement and nervousness.

Next day, in evening at 4 pm, we had a date. It was beginning of November, winters were coming soon, so weather was also pleasant and windy in evening. I chose to wear my favourite dress, a knee length one-piece of maroon colour with floral print. This dress always brightens up my mood. The adrenaline rush and fast heartbeat made my steps hop instead of walk. An ear-to-ear grin captured its permanent space on my face. People in metro must have thought of me as a mad girl or maybe just super excited about something.

The fest was in central park, Connaught Place. I reached Rajiv Chowk metro station and he was already there waiting for me at exit gate. He had reached 10 minutes earlier because of which he admonished me, the way a friend scolds the other for being late and I am always the one who gets reprimanded by my friends.

He said, "Yesterday, someone was saying that be on time, now look who is on time!" He was admonishing and teasing me. I loved how comfortable we got within such short span of time.

For the first time, I was looking at his face intently, trying to connect dots with his pictures. He was wearing a white shirt with green stripes with turquoise-coloured trousers. I must say, he was looking spectacular in that semi formal attire with brown coloured rectangular spectacles. I didn't expect him to be that tall, maybe 6 feet but yes, he was breathtakingly handsome. I tried to control my adrenaline rush and remain calm but only I know how difficult it was especially after seeing him.

He first admonished me for being late and then hugged me from side. My height could reach only till his shoulders. On chat, we had become so comfortable in talking but then in person, it was awkward at first. We silently smiled at each other, twisting our fingers behind our back, exactly opposite of how we were interacting on phone.

We headed to the event. It hadn't started yet so we walked around a bit in central park. Slowly, the wall of awkwardness was shedding and we were there as two good friends having great conversation. We started talking the way we were talking on phone and soon after, there were Nizami brothers singing Qawwali.

The whole environment was mesmerizing with wonderful lighting and their soul satisfying music. The most beautiful part being Sagar sitting beside me. As our bucket of similarity was getting full, I got to know that his favourite song was also "Kunfayakun" and I loved how he enjoyed the music. The Qawaali was soothing my heart and mind. I lost track of time and was completely lost in the moment.

After the event got over, we walked around inner circle of Connaught place, had an ice-cream, and got to know more about each other. He was a shy guy who doesn't wear his heart on his sleeves. I was the one who kept on talking and chit-chatting and he was there sitting beside me looking so adorable with that charming smile patiently listening to everything I was saying. I admire such patient listeners who tolerates my chit chatting. I always want such people around me because of my non-stop talking. But when he spoke, I was intent to listen more, was intent to know him more. He wasn't a playboy kind of guy but rather a genuine one who would take relationships very seriously. The best thing I liked about him was that he didn't want to make any girl his first priority rather his first priority was he himself who aimed to achieve high in his life. The dedication towards his career was what impressed me the most.

I went out on a date with an amazing man who turned into a great friend. We had our day, our new experience exploring through our 20s. I don't know what our future holds but that coincident same timing of installing dating app (which I uninstalled that day) with sudden meeting plan was maybe destiny's way of saying that I wouldn't have to go to poetry festivals alone anymore.

Meet the Co-Authors

Meet the Co-Authors

Deepanshu Joshi

Deepanshu is a 23-year-old writer/ poet hailing from New Delhi, who has a knack for creative experimentation and exploring various genres through his words. His diverse penmanship compliments his skill to pull off his fancy into well-knit tales. His words dwindle between intricate details and character psyche. He is an ardent animal lover and a low-key travel enthusiast. He firmly believes that: "scribe ergo sum ergo".

Aastha Gupta

Aastha is a German language editor by profession. Apart from being a writer, she is a sucker for good poetry and theatre. When she is not working, she likes to build her Urdu vocabulary and binge on content-driven Hindi movies.

Ida Williams

Ida works mostly in the misty days of historical fiction, sometimes wandering around Victorian London or listening to jazz in a 1950s New York café. She is currently creating short stories, online videos and is working on a novel. You can find her at Meadow Afternoon.

Kristofer Bridges

(Kristofer) Osidion is an up-and-coming aspiring author seeking to Network, gain exposure as well as build a following of devoted readers for his manuscripts. History is a huge passion of his and with that being said it's the driving factor for the inspiration and creativity behind the manuscript(s), every manuscript is based on some real world event(s), mythology, or even pseudo history at times.

Dayle Duncan

An author and freelance writer who loves coffee, writes fiction and short stories. Born and raised in South Africa, she is a mother of two wonderful daughters. She is an avid gamer and some of her favourite pastimes are reading, yodelling, playing the piano, and other instruments. Her weakness is chocolate mousse and apple crumble pie.

Khyati Bali

Nothing is black and white in Khyati's world, everything is colour, everything is a rainbow. Khyati is a freelance writer based in Jalandhar. She used to listen to a radio show with her grandfather when she was in 6th standard and that's how she was introduced to the world of storytelling and later fell in love with it. She writes about love, how simple love can be. She wants to convey stories that leave footprints on hearts.

Lily Nielsen

(Elizabeth) Lily Nielsen has been reading and writing for years. What started as school projects, eventually turned into more serious books and Lily has been writing the Mission series since 2017. Failed attempts at contemporary led her to write stories about spy school, madwoman mothers and internet stalking dates. Though still a high school student and training for a life in the performing arts, Lily loves to write and hopes you'll enjoy her stories.

Munmun Aidasani

Munmun Aidasani, Chartered Financial Analyst by profession, hails from city of lakes, Bhopal (India) currently residing in Dubai (U. A. E). She loves wearing many hats. She is an avid and a versatile writer, an author, and a blogger. A dreamer with passion to establish her own benchmark in writing.

When she is not writing, she indulges her children, husband and loved-ones with sumptuous food, with a curious mind trying to witness art in everything possible and in quest of exploring new horizons.

Her inner wisdom of being empathic and caring towards her loved-ones makes her the best human being around. She loves writing fictional as well as reality-based inspiring articles. She wants to spread her wings in each genre and believes in versatility.

She can be reached at -

Instagram: @munmunaidasani

Facebook: @Rising Mom

Email: aidasanimunmun@gmail.com

Violet Evergarden

Violet Evergarden is a 28-year-old author from Johor, Malaysia. A shy and a little introverted author who loves to write during her free time. She has been a writer since 2018 until now. Being busy with her daily routine schedule, writing a romance story is only her escape to her own world of fantasy and wishing to bring joy for the readers.

Amina Hazim

Amina is an eighteen-year-old aspiring writer she has been writing for almost a year now with three novels completed and published on various online reading websites. But her journey doesn't end there, she wants to let the world read about what she writes to put a smile on a person's face who is bleak. Her stories have a unique plot that would keep you coming back for more.

C.L. Williams

C.L. Williams is a multi-genre author from central Virginia. His most recent release is a romance novella titled The Next Step: First Valentine's. In addition to writing his own books, C.L. Williams has also been featured in various anthologies and magazines. When not writing, C.L. Williams is reading and sharing the works of other independent authors.
He can be reached on social media @writer434 and his blog is writer434.wordpress.com.

SELECT RELEASES AND FEATURES

Aspects of Love 1.5 (Love Poem Collection)
META- (Complete) (Poetry)
The Paradox Complex (Poetry)
Shades of BWWM (Anthology includes "The Next Step", "Moving In", and "Unexpected")
Starting Over (Anthology includes "Saved by a Siren"
The Next Step (Romance novella)
The Next Step: First Valentine's (Romance novella)

Ishika Jain

Ishika Jain is a 17-year-old literature enthusiast, who discovered her love for reading and writing when she started obsessing over thriller fictions at a young age. Career-wise she has her eyes set on journalism but having tried her hand at writing, she knows that if she got the right opportunity she will get her own books published one day. She is a well-known author on the eBook platform 'Wattpad' and has received stupendous feedback from her readers for her YA and thriller books.

Nafisa Faruque

Nafisa Faruque is a young and talented writer who enjoys playing with words in symphony to create write-ups. She describes herself as a 17-year-old who is no different than any other of her age. She discovered how fascinating the world of literature can be from a very young age and hopes to keep improving as long as she continues to express herself through her words. More of her work can be found at her Instagram handle @a.urora20.

Ishika Jain

Ishika Jain is an explorer from Delhi who has a never-ending thirst for fascinating stories. By profession, she is working in career guidance domain and by passion, well here she is, in the 'author's bio'. She is a writer who loves to talk, so became a podcaster. She runs her podcast on Spotify named "Soul's Tune". Ishika is an avid reader and loves to travel while listening to amazing podcasts.